"Gina!" Tess called as she entered the rolling wooden walkway of the Funhouse and clutched at the padded walls. "Gina, wait up!"

She hurried through the tilting tunnel and headed for the first of the open balconies, when a sound stopped her in her tracks.

It was a piercing scream that sent slivers of ice sliding down her back.

That scream wasn't a normal part of the Funhouse. It hadn't come from a witch's cackling mouth or a dangling skeleton or a bloody corpse. That scream had been real.

Other Point paperbacks you will enjoy:

point

FUNHOUSE

Diane Hoh

SCHOLASTIC INC.
New York Toronto London Auckland Sydney

ISBN 0-590-43050-5

12 11 10   4 5/9

Printed in the U.S.A.   01

First Scholastic printing, July 1990

FUNHOUSE

Chapter 1

Tess Landers would always remember exactly where she was and what she was doing when The Devil's Elbow roller coaster went flying off its track, shooting straight out into the air and hanging there for a few seconds, before giving in to gravity and plummeting straight to the ground. The crash killed Dade Lewis, destroyed Sheree Buchanan's face, and separated Joey Furman forever from his left leg. And it sent a dozen other roller-coaster riders and ten passersby on the ground to the Santa Luisa Medical Center in screaming ambulances.

Before the crash, Tess was buying a hot dog. With everything. And fries and a large Coke, at a stand not far from where the multicolored cars were making their labored, rattle-clackety climb up the last and most treacherous leg of their journey. The rattle-clatter didn't bother Tess. She had lived in Santa Luisa all of her life and she was used to the sounds of The Boardwalk, the amusement park lining the oceanfront of the Southern California community. Thanks to a mild climate, The Boardwalk was open year-round. Good thing, too, Tess often thought, since without The Boardwalk half the population of their little town would be unemployed. And closing the park, even briefly, would drive most of Santa Luisa's teenagers stark, raving mad. Some worked there, in the shops and arcades and restaurants and booths. Most just played there. What else was there to do in town?

She would always remember what she'd been wearing that night, too. Jeans, boots, and a heavy, white hooded sweater. She'd been waiting patiently for Gina Giambone, her best friend. Gina was always late. Their history teacher, Mr. Dart, teased her nearly every morning. "Hey, Jam-boney, heavy date last night? Looks like you overslept!"

Usually, he was right. Gina dated a lot. Because everyone, girls *and* guys, liked to be around her. She was fun and cute. As short and round as Tess was tall and skinny, with short, dark, curly hair framing her olive-skinned face. Her dark brown eyes were her most outstanding feature. Gina was part of a large Italian family of six kids. Her parents had been married practically forever and seemed very happy, unlike Tess's parents who had recently separated.

Of course Shelley wasn't her real mother. The first Mrs. Landers had died when Tess was nine years old. When she was thirteen, Guy Joe Landers, Sr., had married Shelley, fifteen years his junior. Their marriage had lasted until six weeks earlier, when Shelley had packed her things and left, taking

Tess with her. Now Shelley was about to go gallivanting off to Europe for two weeks with her best friend, Madolyn.

"You can go stay with your father and brother," Shelley had said blithely as she packed. "Or you can hang out here by yourself. Whatever. Lord knows you're old enough at seventeen to take care of yourself."

Well, maybe the Lord knew it and maybe Shelley knew it, but Tess wasn't so sure. The exclusive condominium complex called The Shadows was set deep in the woods, on a hill above town. It was beautiful during the day, but it could be cold and lonely when darkness fell.

But Tess didn't want to go stay with her father and her brother, Guy Joe, Jr. No friend of Shelley's was a friend of her father's now. And Tess couldn't forgive Guy Joe for choosing to live with their father.

"But why?" she had asked him tearfully. "You don't even *like* him!" The two of them, father and son, had never been close. The father had been too busy for the son.

"At least he's my *real* parent," Guy Joe had answered.

Okay, so Shelley was their stepmother, and not such a hot one at that. But at least she could be fun. She talked to Tess as if Tess were actually a real human being, something Tess's father hardly ever did. So when Shelley had offered Tess a bedroom in her new home, and Tess's father hadn't said,

"Please don't go," she'd gone. Thank goodness the condo was large enough that she and Shelley weren't tripping over each other.

"Hi!"

Lost in thought, Tess jumped at Gina's sudden greeting. A blob of yellow mustard squirted from her hot dog, landing smack in the middle of Gina's navy blue wool blazer.

"Oh, darn, I'm sorry!" Tess grabbed a paper napkin and dabbed frantically at the greasy mess. Straight, fair hair flew around her thin face. "You shouldn't sneak up on people like that! You scared me half to death. My hair probably turned white!"

Gina laughed and brushed away the napkin. "Your hair is still the same mousy shade it always was. Anyway, forget about the jacket, okay? It needed a trip to the cleaners before you did your dirty work."

"Well, you're in a pretty good mood tonight," Tess said crankily, because she herself was not. She straightened up, tossing the crumpled napkin into a nearby trash can. "How come?"

Gina grinned. "Because I see Doss Beecham over there, working in the ring toss booth. I think I'm making some progress with him. He's stopped calling me Jam-boney. He actually said, 'Hey, you!' yesterday. Don't you think that's a good sign?"

Tess frowned. "What do you see in that guy, anyway? He looks totally Neanderthal to me. You could have any guy in Santa Luisa and you set your big brown eyes on a bruiser in a white T-shirt who spends more time combing that mess of black hair than he does anything else. I just don't get it!"

Gina shrugged. "I think he's cute. Besides, I feel sorry for him. In case you've forgotten, he used to be one of us. Just because his father lost all their money, everyone looks down on Doss now. Well, I don't. He's the same person he always was." She grinned impishly. "And I intend to make my presence known to him."

"People look down on him," Tess pointed out irritably, "because he's a grouch who walks around looking like the world owes him a living and isn't providing it." Maybe Gina just felt sorry for Doss. Although it wasn't as if the Beecham family were starving to death. They'd managed to hang onto that big brick house of theirs up on the hill. Someone had told her that the Beechams had paid cash for the house, years ago, and all they had to do now was pay the taxes on it. Doss probably paid those. Which meant, Tess guessed, that Doss was no bum. He hadn't let his family get tossed out on the street. That was something in his favor.

"Where's Beak tonight?" Tess asked pointedly.

Another shrug. "Oh, he's around somewhere Probably playing Skee-Ball." She glared at Tess. "And you're about as subtle as a jackhammer. I like Beak, you know that. But Doss is . . . well, he's different. I'm ready for different. Besides," she added, grinning, "how would *you* like to date a guy named Beak?"

The nickname no longer suited Robert Rapp. At

eighteen, his features were perfectly proportioned, which hadn't been the case when he was younger and his nose had been the most prominent feature on his thin, bony face. But the nickname stuck. Tess liked Beak. Except for a penchant for pulling practical jokes, he was nice. She'd always thought he was good for Gina. Apparently, Gina didn't share the thought.

"Maybe Doss will buy me a hot dog," Gina said. "*Without* mustard. So, where's Sam?"

Sam. Pain sliced through Tess's chest. Where was he tonight? And who was he with? "How should I know?" she snapped, turning back to the counter to discard her Coke cup. "I don't own Sam Oliver!"

"Wow!" Doss Beecham commented as he joined them, "who rattled your cage? What'd you do, overdose on sourballs?"

"Never mind," Tess said, embarrassed. She didn't know Doss well enough to behave like a shrew in front of him. "The smell of hot dogs brings out the beast in me."

Doss nodded. "I saw Sam back there. He was alone. You two split?"

She didn't know him well enough to confide in him, either. "Forget it," she said airily. "You guys order your food while I check out the girls' room, okay? Be right back." She didn't feel like hanging around while Gina "got to know" someone who was probably all wrong for her.

But then, who was right for anybody? And how did you know? Her father hadn't been right for Shelley. Just when Tess had thought they were going to have a nice, normal family at last, the marriage had fallen apart. And not too long ago, she had thought Sam Oliver was perfect for her. Wrong, wrong, wrong! The support system her school counselor had said she needed to help her cope with her anxieties was rapidly dwindling. Maybe even disappearing forever.

She pushed open the creaky old metal door to the rest room opposite The Devil's Elbow. Rattle-clatter, clackety-clack. It screeched and groaned its way up the rails over her head. She had ridden it once, when she was nine years old. Never again. She didn't mind some of the other scary rides of The Boardwalk, but the roller coaster had taken her breath away, left her knees feeling like pudding, and kept her heart thudding for hours after the wicked ride was over and she was safely on firm ground.

She washed her hands with cold water and ran a comb through her straight, shoulder-length hair. The face in the mirror was a sober one. Maybe *unhappy* was a better word. Well, why not? Feeling almost totally alone didn't exactly bring a smile to a person's face, did it?

She came out of the girls' room just as The Devil's Elbow reached the pinnacle of its last and highest climb. Reluctant to rejoin Gina and Doss, she leaned against the wall and, tilting her head upward, watched as the roller coaster began its last thundering descent.

She could feel the ride as if she were actually

sitting in one of the cars: The wind slapping her face with such brutal force it stole her breath away, the air heavy with screams and shouts, the sheer terror of the rush downward. The last plunge would seem to take forever, although actually it took only a second, so fast was the speed of the roller coaster. There would be just time enough to appreciate the gentleness of that last curve before coasting into the departure gate.

That was the way it was supposed to happen. That was the way it always happened.

But not this time. This time was horribly, shockingly different.

Because as Tess stood against the wall, the lead car, a brilliant orange trimmed in bright yellow, reached the bottom. But instead of following the track and taking that last gentle curve toward home, it sailed out into the air. The car hung there for a second or two, then plunged downward to The Boardwalk below. It took the remaining eleven cars, some occupied, some empty, with it. The cars hit the ground in rapid sequence. The crash of each one seemed, to Tess's disbelieving ears, louder than the one before it. The screaming that accompanied the fall wasn't the playful kind from moments earlier. These were the screams of terror, and Tess didn't even realize that her own voice was among them.

There was screaming on The Boardwalk, as well. People passing by were struck with large and small chunks of falling metal. Some were hit so hard they were tossed like dolls into nearby booths. A mother ran to snatch her small child from the path of a falling car and both were buried beneath the bright blue metal.

Tess, not breathing, huddled against the wall outside the girls' room, unable to believe what she was seeing and hearing. When the last car had fallen and crashed into bits, a brief, shocked silence filled The Boardwalk.

Some distance away, under the last, gentle curve in The Devil's Elbow, a figure slipped out from underneath the tracks. In black slacks, black turtleneck sweater, and black ski mask, the figure blended into the darkness. But even without darkness, total chaos on The Boardwalk would have made it difficult for anyone to notice the figure, or the long, thick, steel pipe in its hands.

Beneath the ski mask a satisfied smile edged its way around the lips. Then the figure in black turned and loped away.

Tess, shaking her head to clear her mind, looked up just then and the moving shadow caught her eye. It wasn't much more than a blur in the darkness, but something about it struck her as strange. Then she realized what it was. Instead of rushing to The Boardwalk to help, the figure was moving *away* from the scene.

Maybe it was rushing off to call for help?

Then why wasn't it rushing *toward* The Boardwalk, where the nearest phones were located?

And what had it been doing under The Devil's Elbow in the first place?

Before Tess could think of any reasonable answers to those questions, someone called her name, jerking her back to the chaotic reality in front of her.

Chapter 2

They asked for it. They did. They had it coming, all of them. They get no sympathy.

No one suspects. They think it was an accident. Wrong!

It was *so* easy. Climbing up the inside of the roller coaster's white wooden support system, climbing like a monkey in a palm tree. Then jamming the lead pipe up through the rails at exactly the right moment. That old Devil's Elbow took off into space like it was propelled by jet fuel. Easy, it was so easy.

Dade, Sheree, Joey . . . three out of eight, all at the same time. Not bad. Three out of eight's not bad.

Not bad.

Five more to go.

And no one suspects. Because they don't know what I know. And I'm not about to tell. Not until the job is done. Then I'll share my little discovery with all of them.

But right now, it's time to plan the next step.

Chapter 3

As Tess returned abruptly to reality at the sound of her name, the wooden boardwalk vibrated with feet pounding toward the scene of the crash. The air was filled with screams and moans and shouts for help. Tess's ears rang. Her eyes worked at focusing on the scene before her. Booths had been toppled, their wooden sides collapsing like accordions. There was brightly colored metal everywhere, bits and pieces and chunks of it. Some larger chunks partially hid their victims, revealing a skirt and legs or an arm clutching a purse or someone's very curly red hair. A little boy cried out in pain, wanting his mommy.

Tess shuddered. A siren wailing in the distance told her someone had called for help. The person she'd seen beneath The Devil's Elbow? Maybe.

The smells of popcorn and cotton candy and hot dogs were sickening.

Gina and Doss were running toward Tess. "Tess, are you okay?" Gina cried, her face bone-white. "You're not hurt?"

Tess shook her head. But she continued to lean against the wall. She didn't trust her legs to support her all by themselves.

"Were you standing right here when it happened?" Gina's dark eyes, wide with horror, surveyed the disaster scene. "You could have been killed! You sure you're all right?"

"I'm okay. But," she added, pointing shakily to the injured, "they're not. Shouldn't we see if we can help?"

An ambulance shrieked to a halt just beyond the steps to The Boardwalk. Several paramedics in white jumped to the ground and began running, medical equipment in hand.

"They're going to need more than one of those," a deep voice commented in Tess's ear.

It was Sam, in jogging shorts and a red sweatshirt, earphones draped around his neck. His dark hair curled damply across his forehead. "Looks like someone dropped a bomb. What happened?"

"I don't know," Tess answered honestly. A second ambulance arrived, then a third, followed by a black-and-white police car. "The roller coaster just sailed off into the air."

The policemen immediately began trying to disperse the crowd. But no one wanted to leave. People seemed frozen in morbid fascination, their eyes wide, mouths open in disbelief.

"Come on," Tess urged, tugging at Sam's hand. "Let's see if there's anything we can do to help."

The scene that greeted her eyes when she and her friends had pushed through the crowd, made her stomach curl up in fright. Scattered among the bright chunks of broken metal were many of her friends, their bodies crumpled like used paper napkins. Some were unconscious. Some were not as lucky, and cried out in pain.

"There's Sheree Buchanan," Gina whispered, pointing. "There, lying beside the hot-dog stand. I ran into her earlier. She was wearing a purple shirt just like one I bought last week."

Tess moaned low in her throat. Poor Sheree. She would never be the same.

"Dade Lewis is dead!" a girl standing behind Sam cried out. "He's dead!"

A collective gasp of dismay rose up from the crowd.

Dade Lewis? Tess couldn't believe that. Dade was obnoxious, but he was so healthy, so full of life. The girl must be mistaken.

A boy in jeans and a T-shirt ran past Tess, his hand over his mouth, his face sweatshirt-gray. Doss followed him, returning a moment later to say without emotion, "He just came across Joey Furman's leg. Minus Joey. Shook the kid up real bad."

Gina gasped as her hand flew up to cover her mouth. Tess leaned against Sam, all breath completely stolen from her. Joey Furman? He was on the track team, with Guy Joe, Sam, and Beak. Every time she'd seen Joey lately — on The Boardwalk, in town, or at school, he'd been running. And now he'd lost a leg to The Devil's Elbow?

Doss Beecham was an insensitive clod, she thought, as Doss left to help on The Boardwalk.

Talking so matter-of-factly about what had happened to Joey, as if the loss of his leg were no more important than a pimple on his chin! Didn't Doss have any feelings?

She spotted Beak among the volunteers, bending and stooping, his lanky form lifting metal and tossing it aside, as he tried to stay out of the way of the paramedics. His thin face was flushed with exertion and distress.

"There's Beak," she told Gina, nodding toward their friend. She was relieved that he hadn't been a passenger on The Devil's Elbow when it crashed. It was his favorite ride.

Gina simply nodded when Tess mentioned Beak. She was still trying to take in the nightmare around her.

"I'm going with Beecham," Sam told Tess, handing her his earphones. "You stay here with Giambone. And stay *out* of the way."

Ordinarily, Tess's temper would have flared at the command. But nothing tonight was ordinary. Besides, she figured, in this case Sam was probably right. She and Gina could be the most useful by helping to move the crowd back. The policemen weren't having much luck getting onlookers out of the way.

Tess and Gina spent most of the next hour cajoling bystanders, gradually talking them into moving back from the accident scene, leaving the site open for emergency personnel and the cleanup crew.

When the last of the ambulances had departed,

sirens wailing mournfully, and the crowd had wandered off, Tess and Gina collapsed to sitting positions, their backs against a cotton-candy booth left untouched by the disaster. Tess's thin face and Gina's round one were totally devoid of color, their eyes full of pain and shock. Doss and Sam joined them, their own faces and clothes dirty. Sam had a small cut on one hand. They sank down beside the girls and rested their heads against the booth.

Tess's brother, Guy Joe, a tall, broad-shouldered boy with a square, handsome face and deep gray eyes, arrived, his denim cutoffs smeared with grease from his cleanup efforts. Trailing along behind him was Sam's sister Candace, a pale, thin, blonde girl. Candace never wore jeans, and the pink dress she was wearing now was much too large for her, billowing around her like a tent. A heavy hand with an eyebrow pencil made her look far more ferocious than she really was. Tess couldn't understand why Mrs. Oliver, who was tall, beautiful, and very elegant, never took the time to teach her own daughter about clothes and makeup. But tonight, that didn't seem very important.

"Well, at least you weren't on that thing when it went," Guy Joe said to Tess, patting her shoulder awkwardly as he slid to a sitting position beside her. "When I saw the bulletin on television, I thought of you. I know this place is your favorite hangout."

"Guy Joe," Tess said stiffly, still uncomfortable around the brother who had "deserted" her by staying with their father after the separation, "you know I never go near the roller coaster. Haven't since the first time I ever rode it."

"According to the bulletin," her brother argued, running his fingers through his unruly hair, "you didn't have to be on the thing to get clobbered. For all I knew, you could have been creamed by one of the falling cars."

Tess knew he was right. One elderly woman had been tossed into a food booth. Two little boys had been slashed by flying metal chunks, and at least half a dozen other people walking along The Boardwalk at the time of the accident had been sent to the Santa Luisa Medical Center.

"Thanks for worrying about me," she said politely, "but I'm fine."

A tall, big-boned, very pretty girl with thick, blonde shoulder-length hair ran up to them. Dressed in beige silk slacks over a red leotard, she carried her large frame gracefully, moving with quick, light steps across The Boardwalk. When she reached the group, she sank into a crouch beside Gina. Tess noticed that she was careful not to let her silk pants touch the wood, gently bunching them slightly at the knees.

"Isn't this just awful?" the girl breathed, her blue eyes wide. "I can't believe it! My daddy's going to have a stroke! Something like this happening on his beloved boardwalk, it's just terrible! Has anybody seen my little brother?"

The girl was Trudy Slaughter, a classmate of Tess and Gina's, and the "daddy" she spoke of was chairman of the board of directors that ran The

Boardwalk. Trudy was a popular, powerful force at Santa Luisa High, having held at least once, every available office. Tess hadn't voted for her since the day she saw Trudy lose her temper in the school parking lot over an English grade lower than the one she'd been expecting. Seeing Trudy violently ripping at sheets of paper and slamming her books against the windshield of a car had not been a pretty sight. It had given Tess chills, and she knew she'd seen a side of Trudy that not many other people had witnessed.

"I saw Tommy," Gina said, referring to the brother Trudy had asked about. "He's fine. He's with one of Beak's kid sisters. They weren't hurt, either."

"I was at ballet class," Trudy breathed, "when we all heard this horrible sound. Debbie Wooster thought it was an earthquake and ran screaming into the bathroom. But Madame Souska said it wasn't, because the chandelier wasn't shaking. She let us turn on the radio and that's how we heard. We were excused from practice, can you believe that? She never excuses us for anything!" Trudy's chest heaved in a heavy sigh. "I suppose that means we'll have to make it up another time."

"Poor thing," Tess said sarcastically, too tired to ignore Trudy's callousness. "And yes, we're all fine, thanks for asking."

Trudy blushed. "Well, I can *see* that! I heard about Dade, though. I can't believe it. How did it happen, anyway?"

"No one knows," Guy Joe said wearily. "Maybe a loose rail."

"I saw someone," Tess said quietly.

Everyone's eyes focused on her. But she could tell that her words hadn't registered. "Under The Devil's Elbow," she added, flushing because she hated being the center of attention, and already wishing she hadn't said anything. "Right after the accident. Running away."

"Well, don't keep us in suspense," Trudy said anxiously. "Who *was* it?"

"You saw someone?" Sam asked quietly, leaning forward to peer into Tess's face. "Running away?"

Tess nodded. "I think so. It was awfully dark and I couldn't see very well. But there was something . . ." A lack of conviction forced her words to trail off weakly.

No one said anything for a moment. They think I imagined it, she thought resentfully. I never should have said anything.

Then Doss surprised her by asking calmly, "Who did it look like, Tess? Was it someone we know?" He seemed to be assuming that she hadn't imagined the shadow.

Sending him a grateful glance, she admitted reluctantly, "No, not really. But I thought . . . well, I thought there was something familiar about the way it moved."

"The way what moved?" Beak asked as he joined them. Sweat from his work with the cleanup crew streaked his thin, intense face. Swiping at it with the sleeve of his navy blue sweatshirt, he sank down beside Gina.

"Tess thinks she saw someone running away from The Devil's Elbow," Gina told him. Although she said *thinks*, Tess felt that Gina, too, believed her, and she sent her best friend a warm smile.

"Running *away*?" Beak asked, leaning back against the booth. "Why would someone be running *away*? Are you hinting that you think someone *did* something to The Devil's Elbow? Deliberately caused the accident?"

That thought hadn't even crossed Tess's mind. Wide-eyed she stared at Beak. "No, I . . ."

Sam interrupted her. "Maybe you should talk to the police. Tell them what you saw."

Tess looked doubtful. What could she possibly tell them? That she'd seen a shadow? Wouldn't they laugh at her?

"Relax," Doss said lazily. "Chalmers will look into it. That's his job. If he finds even a hint of tampering, then Tess can go to him with what she saw."

Sam laughed. "Chalmers? Our distinguished police chief? He couldn't find his own nose without a mirror. Besides, the board got him elected in the first place, to make sure their precious Boardwalk was protected. If he does find anything, whether it was faulty equipment or actual tampering, he's not going to announce it publicly. Either way, it'd be bad for business."

"Oh, Sam," Gina scolded, "you're so cynical! The

board wouldn't hide something like that. And the police would never cover it up."

Sam shrugged. "We'll see."

An uncomfortable silence followed. Then Tess asked, "Anyone know who called the paramedics?" Maybe it had been the shadow she'd seen. That would explain why it had been there and she could forget about it.

Doss nodded. "Martha did," he said, referring to an elderly woman who ran the shooting gallery. "I never knew she could move so fast. The minute that thing took off, Martha raced for the nearest phone."

Of course, Tess told herself. Because that was what you *did* in an emergency. You ran *toward* the phone, not away from it.

Unless you weren't interested in getting help.

Unless you were only interested in running away. Because you had good reason to run away.

Telling herself she was letting her imagination do some pretty fancy running, Tess pushed all thought of the shadow out of her tired, aching mind. All she wanted to do now was go home and crawl under the covers and sleep, and forget about this dreadful, horrible night.

As if it could ever be forgotten¹

Chapter 4

I found it in the attic. I was looking for ski clothes.
Found no ski clothes. Found the book, instead. A
journal. A little red book, hidden in the bottom of
an old trunk. The name on the front, in cheap gold
letters, was LILA O'HARE.

O'Hare? No O'Hares in this family. None in Santa
Luisa, for that matter.

I read that journal. Took me all day, but I read
it. Every page. Hot day, stuffy attic with its tiny
windows and sloping walls and smells of cedar and
mothballs. Sat there all day, sweating and reading.

Glad I read it. Even though it changed everything. When I finished reading it, I knew that nothing would ever be the same again.

But I'm not sorry I read it.

The journal was written by this woman named
Lila, who was married to a guy named Tully O'Hare
who owned The Boardwalk. Reading that seemed
weird, because I'd never thought about who owned
The Boardwalk before my father and his friends

bought it. Now I knew. Someone named Tully O'Hare.

Lila and Tully ran The Boardwalk together. Very happy, the O'Hares were. Pretty boring stuff, but I read it anyway. Nothing better to do.

Then suddenly the entries changed.

I wish someone could help us. We can't pay the back taxes on The Boardwalk. Tully's worried sick. He's afraid we're going to lose everything.

What would we do without The Boardwalk? It's our whole life. Tully's granddaddy built it and it's all we've got. I don't know what Tully will do if it's taken away from us.

We were both so excited about the baby coming. We've waited and hoped for so long. Now Tully is afraid we won't be able to take care of our child.

He's going to the bank to see Buddy about a loan. Maybe that will save us.

Who was Buddy? Was there a banker in town named Buddy? Not that I knew of.

Turns out, there were a *lot* of things I didn't know.

Chapter 5

When Tess announced that she was going home, Sam insisted on walking her to the parking lot. Almost empty now, it seemed strangely eerie and quiet. As uncomfortable as she felt around Sam after their fight earlier in the week, she was glad she wasn't alone.

Lights began flickering off at The Boardwalk. Someone had made the decision to close early. Good idea. Tess shuddered. Who could have a good time there tonight?

Sam moved forward to stand beside her. A breeze off the ocean picked up stray strands of his dark, wavy hair and lifted them gently. "So, Shelley take off yet?" he asked brusquely.

Oh, no. Were they going to have *that* discussion again? Their argument had been about Shelley. When Sam found out that Shelley was leaving for Europe, he'd made some snide remarks about her abilities as a parent. Because Shelley had wanted Tess when no one else seemed to, Tess had defended her stepmother. The argument had escalated, and

Sam had left her house in a fury. She didn't want to get into that again, especially not when she was feeling so shocked and shaken.

"Yes," she mumbled, turning toward her little blue car, "she's gone. Left around five o'clock." Would Shelley have gone if she'd known about The Devil's Elbow? Probably.

"Then I'll drive you home," Sam said in that commanding voice she hated. "You can come back and pick up your car tomorrow."

It would be nice, when she was feeling so sick inside, to let Sam take over. But that would just reinforce his notion that she needed looking after. Even though sometimes — like that night — she wouldn't have minded letting him decide things for her, she certainly wouldn't admit that to *him*. If he wanted someone to take care of, let him buy a puppy!

"I can drive myself home, thank you very much," she said, her voice as cool as the night air.

"You are so stubborn!" he said heatedly, throwing his hands up in the air in disgust. "You never give an inch!"

That seemed funny to Tess and she almost laughed. She'd been giving inches all of her life. People told her what to do and she did it, because it was easier than arguing. If she was arguing now, with Sam, maybe it was because doing what people told her hadn't worked out so well. Just when she'd thought she was finally going to have a happy family, like other people, her father had said, "We're divorcing," and that was that.

So if she'd been giving Sam a hard time lately, maybe it was because she was getting just a little tired of having other people make her decisions for her.

"I'm going home," she said flatly, opening the door of her car.

"Fine! Great! You do that!" And he stalked away, broad shoulders jerking in anger with each stride.

Watching him go, she was unpleasantly surprised to discover that she was analyzing his walk, comparing it to the movements of the figure she'd seen running away from The Boardwalk. Afraid that he would turn suddenly and see her watching him, she ducked into her car and settled behind the wheel. If Sam *had* been running under The Devil's Elbow, he would have said so when she'd mentioned what she'd seen. He would have said casually, "Oh, that was me. That's the route I take when I jog." And that would have been the end of it. She would have put the figure out of her mind completely.

But Sam hadn't said that. So it hadn't been him.

Then who *was* it? And why had they run away, instead of rushing to The Boardwalk to help?

Maybe the person *had* helped out. It suddenly occurred to Tess, as she headed up the hill toward home, that the figure she'd seen could easily have joined the crowd of volunteers without her knowing it. After all, she hadn't recognized the person, so how could she say whether or not they had returned to the accident and pitched in?

She'd been jumping to conclusions, as usual. She

had no real reason to believe sinister things about that figure. Might as well put it out of her mind right now.

She had always loved the drive home, up the hill. Random house lights scattered throughout the woods on both sides of the road eased the darkness, like candlelight in a dark room. It had always seemed peaceful, even romantic.

But not tonight. Not with those terrible screams echoing in her ears.

At the top of the hill, she took a sharp right turn into the long, tree-lined driveway leading to The Shadows, the exclusive condominium complex she and Shelley called home now. Their unit was all the way at the back, overlooking a lush green valley. Tess loved the daytime view, but at night it seemed isolated and lonely. This would be her first night alone in the house and she wasn't looking forward to it. Shelley's timing was the worst! Why did she have to leave for Europe on the very night that the worst disaster in Santa Luisa's history had taken place?

The patio beside their carport was surrounded on three sides by tall, thick oleander bushes, their narrow green leaves swaying in the night breeze. A small, black, metal gate separated the carport from the patio, which sat directly outside the condo's kitchen. Tess hurried from the car to the back door, unlocked it and went inside, quickly flipping on the kitchen light switch as she entered the house.

It seemed so empty. No Shelley fixing a drink in

the kitchen, no loud jazz music blasting through the rooms, no coat, purse, car keys, scarf, magazines, and newspaper left in a trail behind Shelley as she advanced from one room to another.

Tess swallowed hard. Even when Shelley was in town, she wasn't home that many evenings. What was so different about tonight?

What was different was that something atrocious had happened and Tess wanted someone there to share her pain.

While flooding the kitchen with light made the room feel a bit more friendly, it also seemed to magnify the wide, gaping blackness of the big picture windows over the double sink and the French doors opposite the breakfast nook. Shelley didn't believe in curtains or drapes. She said she liked to "bring the outdoors in," and usually added, "where it belongs," which Tess found funny.

It didn't seem the least bit funny tonight. Tess couldn't have said why, but the bare, black windows left her feeling raw and exposed.

When the phone shrilled, she jumped, banging her elbow on the kitchen counter and dropping her purse. Her lipstick fell out and rolled under the oval wooden table in the breakfast nook.

It was Gina calling. "Just wanted to make sure you got home in one piece. You seemed pretty rattled."

Tess laughed nervously. "I guess I still am, a little. Aren't you?"

"I feel just horrible. All those people hurt. Poor

Joey! And Sheree! And then there's Dade . . ."

They both fell silent. Then Gina said, "Are you all alone or is Sam playing bodyguard? I saw him leave with you."

Tess switched on the breakfast nook chandelier, a hanging fixture with lights shaped like candles ensconced in copper holders. Shelley had left the sink full of dishes, as always. Tess hooked the black rubber phone grip over her shoulder and began loading the dishwasher as she talked. "I'm alone. Shelley's off to sunny Italy. And I didn't feel like dealing with Sam tonight." She paused, before adding seriously, "Gina, hasn't The Boardwalk been in business for about a hundred years?"

"Give or take a year or two. Why?"

"And there's never been an accident there before tonight, right? Not a really bad one, I mean." Gina's father, like most of the parents Tess knew, including her own father, was on the amusement park's board of directors. And since Mr. Giambone, unlike Tess's father, actually *talked* to his daughter, Gina might know something about The Boardwalk's history.

Gina thought for a minute. "Not on The Devil's Elbow," she answered. "But something might have happened in the Funhouse. Don't know what, exactly, but I remember my dad saying something about it once. Whatever it was, it happened before our dads and their friends bought The Boardwalk and remodeled it. I can ask him about it if you want me to. Why? What's up?"

She's already forgotten that I told her I saw something, Tess thought, annoyed. Maybe I'm just jealous of her ability to shut out bad things. No wonder she's never nervous! "Well, don't you think it's kind of weird?" She tipped a glass half full of milk into the sink and rinsed it under the faucet. "I mean, after all these years, all of a sudden there's this terrible accident? Whatever happened in the Funhouse couldn't have been as bad as this, or we'd all have heard about it. So why did something so awful suddenly happen?"

"Tess. If you were almost a hundred years old, don't you think you might break down a little, too?"

"Maybe. But I hope things wouldn't be falling *off* me! Tell the truth, Gina. Do you really think it was an accident?"

She could almost see the frown on Gina's face as her thick, dark eyebrows drew together the way they did when Gina concentrated. "It's that shadow you saw under The Devil's Elbow, isn't it, Tess? That's what's spooking you. So, what are you thinking? That someone put a bomb on the rails? Santa Luisa isn't exactly terrorist territory!

"Tess, you got this idea from Sam, didn't you? Did he say something to you after you left here? You know how cynical he is! Why do you listen to him when he's saying gloomy things?"

"Gina, I didn't *get* this idea from Sam. *I'm* the one who saw something, remember? With my own eyes."

Gina wasn't giving in. "Why don't you just wait and see what the police come up with? I'll bet my new purple blouse that it was just a worn-out rail in the tracks. You'll see."

Her new purple blouse, Tess remembered, was exactly like the one Sheree Buchanan had been wearing earlier. Tess didn't want it. "No, thanks. No bet. I'm not in a gambling mood."

They might have continued arguing, but Tess's eyes, scanning the white brick floor for her lipstick, spotted something else. A piece of crisp white paper was sticking out from underneath the French doors. Had Shelley dropped something on her way out? It would be just like her.

Telling Gina she'd see her tomorrow, Tess hung up. Then she bent to pick up the piece of paper.

It was folded once, into a small white square. She turned it over. Scrawled across the front, in bright purple Magic Marker, was her name.

She didn't recognize the writing. It wasn't Shelley's, she was sure of that. Besides, she told herself, Shelley wasn't the type to leave notes for people when she went somewhere. She just went.

Her breathing slightly uneven, Tess leaned against the counter as she unfolded the note.

The words, like her name, were written in that same vivid purple. Her eyes wide, her hands beginning to shake, Tess read:

> *Dade and Sheree went up the hill,*
> *With Joey right behind them,*
> *Now Dade is dead and Sheree's ill,*
> *And Joey's leg can't find him.*

If Dade was one, and Sheree two,
And Joey number three,
Who will be next? Could it be you?
Why don't we wait and see?

Chapter 6

I delivered my little note to Tess. I hope it shakes her up. A lot. Serve her right.

She doesn't even know why. No one does. No one knows what I found in the attic. I'll tell them when I'm good and ready.

The little red book held secrets. I kept reading, that hot, sticky day a few weeks ago, before the air had turned cool and crisp.

After Tully O'Hare went to the bank to get a loan from his friend Buddy, Lila O'Hare wrote:

I can't believe it! Buddy turned us down. He and Tully have been friends since grade school. Now Tully is drowning and Buddy won't throw him a rope.

Why not?

And what are we going to do now?

Bad Buddy the banker. Who *was* he? If there was a banker in town named Buddy, I'd never heard of him. Maybe he'd dumped the nickname. Maybe he'd dumped the bank. The journal was dated a long time ago. Years ago. Lots of things could have changed in that time.

The next entry explained the one before it.

We found out why Buddy turned us down at the bank. He and a bunch of his friends want The Boardwalk! As an investment. They say they have the funds to turn it into a huge money-making proposition. And we don't.

But it's ours! It's all we have. They can't take it from us, can they?

Why was I so sure the answer to that question was yes, they can. Maybe from watching my father make so many deals over the years. He had the money and the power, and he always won.

I was right. Because the next entry read:

It's gone. The Boardwalk. Buddy and his friends now own it. Tully is devastated. So am I.

What will happen to us now? How will we take care of our baby when it gets here?

The next few pages were blank.

Chapter 7

The blood in Tess's veins turned to sleet as she read, and then reread, the note's purple words.

Who will be next? What did that mean? Next, as in, next after Dade and Sheree and Joey? As in, look what happened to *them*?

Sheree's ruined face swam before Tess's eyes. Then Dade's lifeless body did the same, and Joey's leg . . .

Her knees, which had been threatening all evening to buckle, did so now. Her body slid down the cabinet until it collided gently with the floor. She still held the note in her hands, clenched so tightly her knuckles were blue-white. Unable to stop herself, she glanced down at the little square of paper again.

The purple letters hadn't rearranged themselves into a friendlier message. The words still conveyed the same ugly, threatening meaning.

Her mind, fogged by shock and exhaustion, fought to make sense of it. Was it a joke? Who did she know with such a bizarre sense of humor? And if it wasn't a joke, then what was it?

She read it one more time. How could the meaning be mistaken? Wasn't it proof that what had happened tonight at The Boardwalk was no accident? Or could someone with a twisted sense of humor simply be using the crash to scare her? Hinting that something else equally horrible might be in the works, just to tease her?

No. That would be too cruel. No one she knew had such a sick sense of humor.

Okay, then. How about someone she *didn't* know? Was that possible? There *were* people like that, weren't there? People who thrived on tragedy and horror and used it for their own benefit? Like people who read about kidnappings and then send a fake ransom note to the parents? Couldn't the person who had written this purple poem be someone like that?

Tess stood up. She kept her eyes away from the blackness of the windows and the French doors. The person who had written the poem could be watching. Watching her. His or her sick, horrid eyes could, at this very instant, be fixed on her building.

I shouldn't stay here tonight, Tess thought nervously. Her father's big, very solid, well-protected house beckoned. She'd be safe there. Miserable, especially if her father was home. He'd start right in on her about Shelley, for sure. But at least, she'd be safe.

Or she could call Sam. He'd come and stay with her. But she was so rattled by the accident and now the note that she'd probably throw herself into his arms. And that would be a major mistake!

With shaking fingers, she dialed her father's telephone number. She let it ring eight or nine times. No answer.

Why wasn't Guy Joe home? He couldn't still be at The Boardwalk. Maybe Trudy had talked him into giving her a ride home. If she had, who knew what time Guy Joe would finally call it a night? Trudy didn't have a curfew. Her parents were very busy socially and seldom home. So Trudy saw no need to be, either.

If I have to spend the night alone, Tess decided, I'd rather spend it here, in my own house, surrounded by my own things. Besides, she told the grandfather clock as she passed it, that stupid note was probably a joke. A bad one, but still a joke.

Locking all the doors and windows was the first step. Then, feeling just a tiny bit silly but willing to take no chances, she pushed the heavy oval table in front of the French doors. That done, she thought about calling Gina to read her the note, but decided against it. It was too late. Why wake up the whole Giambone family? Especially since Gina would probably just confirm what Tess had already decided: that the note was a rotten joke

But when Tess left the kitchen, she didn't turn off the light The note still in her hand, she made her way through the spacious condo, flipping on light switches as she went. All of the rooms were large and airy, decorated by Shelley in French coun try style, the walls painted a soft gray-blue or wallpapered in tiny floral prints. The furniture was comfortably cushioned in blue-and-rose plaid. Shelley had added wicker baskets, hanging plants at the windows, and an abundance of white floor-to-ceiling bookcases. This home was prettier, warmer, and cozier than the Landers' mansion.

But as Tess passed from kitchen to dining room to wide, open, French-doored living room, she suddenly found herself wondering how she would defend herself if someone broke into the house. She'd never had such thoughts before. They made her skin feel as if something ugly were crawling on it.

Picking out a heavy brass poker from the set beside the white brick fireplace, she settled, still fully dressed, on the roomy couch. Covering her legs with a quilted throw, she turned on the television set for company and positioned the poker at her side. She wouldn't sleep. She couldn't. She'd stay alert tonight and sleep during the day. People didn't break into houses in broad daylight, did they?

But the horror of the night had exhausted her and the need for sleep won out over her resolve.

When she finally gave in and closed her eyes, every light in the house was still blazing brightly.

Chapter 8

Tess awoke, stiff and headachey, to sunlight streaming in through the French doors and a cartoon blaring at her from the television set. When the memory of the previous night's events flooded back into her mind, she made a decision.

Fifteen minutes later, after pulling on a full, flowered skirt and a white short-sleeved blouse, and clipping her hair on top of her head with a wide gold barrette, she grabbed her purse and the note and drove straight to the police station.

Chief Chalmers wasn't there.

"Doesn't come in on Sundays," the desk sergeant informed her. A heavyset balding man with a mustache and round eyeglasses, he sat with his feet up on the desk, which was littered with papers. No one else was in the small, wood-paneled front office. Dying plants lined the windowsills behind the policeman and half filled coffee cups seemed to be everywhere.

"Sunday's his day of rest," the desk sergeant continued. He shook his head. "Not today, though.

Today's he's seeing to that mess over there at The Boardwalk." Another shake of his balding head. "Terrible thing, terrible thing."

"I need some help," Tess said, extending the note toward him.

"You got a problem, little lady?" he asked, swinging his feet to the floor and sitting up straight. His light blue uniform was clean except for a tiny coffee stain on his navy blue tie. "What's the matter, you missing a boyfriend? Nah, that can't be it. Fellow'd have to be crazy to walk out on a pretty little thing like you." He smiled at her, obviously expecting her to return the smile.

She didn't. Standing up very straight, grateful that she'd worn her black heels, she said crisply, "I'm not little. And my problem isn't a boy. It's this note." She tossed the white piece of paper onto his desk. "Someone slid it under my door last night. I need to know what I should do about it."

He picked it up. "What's this? A love note?"

"Not exactly. Could you look at it, please?" The emptiness of the station wasn't very reassuring. Didn't Santa Luisa have more law enforcement than this? Where was everyone? Did they think criminals took Sundays off, like Chief Chalmers?

She watched as he read the note. Now, maybe he would take her seriously. The note should worry him, shouldn't it? It had certainly worried *her*.

But it didn't seem to worry him. "This thing doesn't make any sense at all. And it looks like a kid's handwriting to me. Written in crayon, right?"

"Magic Marker." Did he think crazy people who

wrote threatening notes used only the finest writing tools? "It wasn't written by a kid," she insisted. "Don't you recognize those names?"

"Sure. They're the kids hurt last night. Devil's Elbow. Bad business, over there. Terrible accident."

Tess leaned forward, placing the palms of her hands on his desk. "But doesn't that note sound like the crash wasn't an accident? And doesn't it sound like the person writing it was warning that there might be other accidents?"

The man reread the note, pursing his lips in concentration. When he'd finished, he looked up and said, "I don't see that here. Where does it say that?"

Impatiently, Tess pointed to the words *Who will be next?* "There! Isn't that a warning?"

"Could be, I guess. Hard to say. Could be a joke. Someone trying to scare you. You have a fight with your boyfriend lately?"

Stunned by the question, Tess fought the telltale flush that crept up her cheeks.

"I thought so." The policeman nodded with satisfaction.

As if, she thought bitterly, he'd just solved the crime of the century.

"Look, miss, I'm not trying to give you a hard time. It's just that we get stuff like this in here all the time. Young fella gets mad, says things he doesn't mean, the girl comes in all worried and upset and we have to calm her down. Lots of times, the guy writes notes. Never amounts to a hill of beans."

"My boyfriend," Tess said coldly, "would never

scare me like this! He would never write a crazy note like this."

The frown on his face then told her she'd worn out her welcome. "It's like this, miss. Chief Chalmers has his hands full right now with this Boardwalk business. But soon as he comes in, I'll give him your note and see what he thinks. You can rest assured that if there's anything connecting this note with that crash last night, the chief will take care of it. He'll probably call you. Okay?" And with that, he turned away from her, picking up a sheet of paper and studying it.

Tess knew she'd been dismissed. And she hadn't accomplished anything.

"Could I have my note back, please?" It suddenly seemed important to have it. That was probably the only way to keep it from sailing straight into the wastebasket the minute she turned her back.

A dubious shake of the man's head. "I'd better keep it, miss. We intend to follow up on this, I promise you that." Opening his desk drawer, he dropped the note into a jumble of papers.

She'd have to leave. *Without* her note.

"It's not that I don't believe there was a note, Tess," Gina said half an hour later, as they shared a booth at Kim's, an ice-cream shop not far from Gina's house. "I do. You wouldn't make up something like that." Wearing the red silk dress she'd worn earlier to church, she sat opposite Tess, who was toying with the straw sticking up out of her vanilla milkshake. "It's just that it *has* to be a joke.

A really mean one, but a joke. I hate to see you get all upset over it."

Tess began tapping her long-handled spoon on the Formica table. "I told you exactly what it said. Doesn't it sound to you like it means the crash was no accident?"

But she knew it was hopeless. Gina's cheerful, uncomplicated way of looking at things didn't include deliberate acts of terror or threatening notes. That was just the way she was. Which, Tess decided in all fairness, was probably why she smiled more than most people. There weren't any scary demons or ghosts running around in her head.

"Let's wait and see what the police say, okay?" Gina urged. "And by the way, I did ask my dad about any other accidents at The Boardwalk," she added in an obvious effort to make peace. "He hates talking about stuff like that, so it didn't make him very happy."

Like father, like daughter, Tess thought drily.

"But he did say some guy committed suicide in the Funhouse a long time ago. Hung himself."

"Yuck! No kidding? No wonder I was never crazy about that place. Who was it?"

Gina stirred her Coke with her straw. "Daddy wouldn't say. And Mom made us change the subject."

"I wonder why we never heard about it before?"

Gina shrugged. "It happened a long time ago. Before we were born. I guess it's not the kind of thing people like to talk about."

As they left the restaurant, Gina tried one more

time to cheer up Tess. "Let's just wait and see what Chief Chalmers comes up with before you start running around town like Henny-Penny, shouting that the sky is falling. Okay?"

"Just don't be surprised," Tess said darkly, "if it turns out that I'm right. And I *am* going to say I told you so."

Gina laughed. "Of course you are. Anyway, we probably won't hear anything about it until tomorrow. So, since you're so jittery, why not stay at my house tonight? No school tomorrow, did you know that?"

Tess hadn't known. She was relieved to hear it. The atmosphere in school would have been grim.

"The school board gave everyone the day off out of respect for Dade," Gina continued. "We could see a movie this afternoon. Something really funny, to take your mind off all this stuff."

More relief. Tess had been reluctant to invite herself to stay at Gina's, even for just one night. The Giambone house was already packed to the rafters with kids and toys and bicycles and pets. She usually stayed overnight only when at least one Giambone was doing the same at someone else's house. "Thanks," she said gratefully, "that'd be fun."

It almost was. The movie was funny, and she felt perfectly safe in a theater full of people.

And what could hurt her at the Giambones'? The house, messy and cluttered, noisy and busy, shouldn't have been relaxing, but it always was. Gina's parents welcomed her warmly, the smaller children gave her hugs and begged her to read to them, which she did. And The Devil's Elbow crash wasn't mentioned once.

So Tess should have felt blissfully safe. She should have slept like a baby all night in the big, crowded house.

But she didn't. Because vivid purple words kept dancing in front of her eyes. *Who will be next? It could be you . . . it could be you . . . it could be you . . .*

Chapter 9

She went to the police with my poem. I was watching. I watched her house all night. Silly girl. The police probably think she's loony-tunes. Laughed at her, I'll bet!

Have to hand it to her, though. I thought she'd split when she got my note. She didn't. Stayed right there. Had every light in the condo on, though. The place looked like one giant light bulb!

She stayed at Giambones' last night. Okay by me. Plenty of time. After all, a few weeks ago I didn't even know what I know now.

Until I read Lila O'Hare's journal.

After that bunch of blank pages following the entry about losing The Boardwalk, she began writing again.

My Tully is gone. I know people are saying that what he did was cowardly, but Tully was no coward. He did it for me and the baby. He didn't know, that poor, sweet man, that the insurance company wouldn't pay off in a suicide case.

How am I going to take care of our baby when it comes?

The man was *dead?* That was pretty gruesome. I wondered if those guys who took The Boardwalk from him felt guilty. Maybe not. I knew what my own father would say. He'd say, "Look, the guy couldn't hack it. Is that *my* fault?"

Well, yes, actually, I guess it could have been. *If* my father had been in on the deal. I hoped he hadn't, but after all, the journal was in this trunk in this attic in this house and I had a sneaking suspicion that meant something. Lila went on:

Buddy came to see me. He said I shouldn't worry, that he'd take care of everything, that they all felt guilty about buying The Boardwalk, that they never thought it would drive Tully to suicide.

They didn't buy The Boardwalk. They stole it!

But I have to let Buddy help me. I have no choice.

She was going to let this creep help her out, after what he'd done. She must really be desperate.

Tiny little hammers tattooing the inside of my skull made me put the journal down.

Chapter 10

When Tess went home the next day, Gina insisted she take one of the Giambone cats with her. "For company," she said. "Take Trilby. She's the most affectionate. She has a thing for laps and she loves to be petted. You can keep her until Shelley gets back."

"Is Trilby trained as an attack cat?" Tess joked, in an effort to calm the nerves that were stretched taut from uncertainty and lack of sleep. What had that purple note meant? And who had written it? And *why*? Had it really been just a sick joke?

The cat was beautiful, a sleek Siamese with clear blue eyes. She purred with gratitude when she was allowed to lounge in Tess's lap all the way home.

Tess had barely had time to change into jeans and a yellow sweatshirt when the phone rang. It was Gina. "Listen, I know you're not going to be crazy about this idea," she warned, "but just hear me out, okay? My dad asked me this morning if I could get a bunch of kids together to go to The

Boardwalk sometime this week. Just to show people that it's safe, you know?"

But *is* it? Tess wondered.

"I thought," Gina continued, "since we have the day off, this afternoon would be a good time. I've already talked to Beak and Sam and they think it's a good idea. Sam said he'd call Guy Joe. And I think Trudy and Candace might come, too. Trudy told me she was planning to sleep all day, but when I told her Guy Joe was coming, she changed her mind. And Sam said he'd bring Candace."

"I don't want to go down there," Tess protested. The oval table was still firmly pressed up against the French doors, a reminder that Saturday night's note hadn't been imagined. If the author had had something to do with the roller coaster crash, he might be hanging around The Boardwalk. Returning to the scene of the crime. Didn't criminals do that sort of thing? "Why can't we do something else?"

"C'mon, Tess, please? First of all, there *isn't* anything else to do. Secondly, my dad's worried about what the accident will do to business on The Boardwalk, and I don't blame him. Look, he hardly ever asks me for anything. I don't want to turn him down." Gina's voice took on a stubborn note. "I'm going over there this afternoon. You coming?"

Tess hesitated. Gina's father had always been kind to Tess. If he was really worried, she should help out.

"Okay, I'll come. What time?"

"Oh, great! Listen, we'll just hang out in the

Funhouse, okay? No rides, not when you're so up-tight. I wouldn't torture you by forcing you on The Dragon's Breath or Helicopter Hell. But the Funhouse is perfectly safe. We're meeting at the entrance at two, but I thought maybe you could pick me up?"

"Sure." The Funhouse wasn't *always* safe, Tess thought grimly. Someone had committed suicide in there, a long time ago. But then, it wasn't as if someone had attacked him in there. He'd taken his own life.

"The Funhouse isn't my favorite place to be," Tess said before she hung up, "but at least it doesn't have any windows so it won't have a view of The Devil's Elbow. That's about the only place on The Boardwalk that doesn't. So maybe it won't be so grim."

Gina laughed. "If it was grim," she teased, "they'd have to call it the Grimhouse. And nobody would visit it and the whole boardwalk would go out of business and we'd all be poor."

Tess hung up.

And realized immediately that she'd forgotten to ask Gina if her father had heard anything about the investigation. The police should know something by now, shouldn't they?

She'd ask this afternoon. Beak might have heard something if Gina hadn't. His parents were on the board of directors, too, as were Sam's and Trudy's. And Chalmers would probably go to the board with whatever he found before he shared it with the general public.

Too bad she couldn't call her own father. Well, it wasn't that she *couldn't*. She just didn't *want* to. If she told him how nervous the note had made her, he'd tell her she was being illogical and unreasonable and overreacting.

She'd rather find out what she needed to know from Gina or Guy Joe or any one of her friends. They wouldn't lecture her. Before she left, she gave Trilby a small bowl of water and a dish of the cat food Gina had sent with her.

Gina hadn't heard a thing about the investigation and neither had anyone else. When Tess complained, Sam lifted one dark eyebrow as if to say, "See? What did I tell you?"

The roller coaster frame had been roped off and tagged with large cardboard signs commanding NO ENTRY and STAY OUT! and CLOSED FOR REPAIRS. Everything else on The Boardwalk remained open. And just as Mr. Giambone had feared, few people were taking advantage of the fact. After all, something terrible had happened there. Something terrible could easily happen again. Why take a chance?

Tess understood that feeling. It was slinking around in her own head, tugging at her and making it impossible for her to relax. The purple note had mentioned a *next*. But it hadn't said when to expect it. Which meant that today couldn't be ruled out, could it?

Gina, trying to keep everyone's mind off the crash, chattered cheerfully as the group headed for the Funhouse. A bright red scarf tied around her dark curls, she trotted purposefully ahead of them in knee-length red shorts and a red-and-white flowered shirt. The sight of her, looking as if she hadn't a care in the world, should have perked up Tess's spirits, but it didn't. She had already begun gnawing on the fingernails it had taken her months to grow. She shouldn't have come. Keeping her eyes averted from the silent Devil's Elbow frame didn't keep the screams and moans and cries for help from echoing in her head. And she found herself continually looking over her shoulder, consumed by a creepy feeling that someone was watching her.

The Funhouse was a long, narrow tunnel built in an L shape, the foot of the L built out over the beach and supported by wooden stilts. The dark wooden structure contained several small areas of open railings dividing one passageway from another, where people could momentarily relax and enjoy the scenery and salt air before going on to the next challenge. Tess, her stomach rebelling after conquering the challenges of the rolling wooden walkway and then the tossing and tilting of a moving padded tunnel, took advantage of the second of these open balconies to catch her breath and settle her insides. Gina, Trudy, and Candace went on ahead to the third event, a nylon-padded tunnel whose footing consisted solely of heavy metal chain links.

Tess breathed in the cool air and tried to relax. But it was impossible. She was uncomfortable being anywhere near The Boardwalk, and she couldn't stop thinking about the man who had committed suicide in the Funhouse.

"You sick?" Guy Joe asked suddenly, coming up beside her. His yellow sweatshirt matched hers. But his complexion wasn't green, as she was sure hers must be. He looked tanned and healthy, as always. His stomach was stronger than hers.

"Uh-uh. Just catching my breath. You go ahead with the others." She should tell him about the note. But if he believed it was really a threat, he'd just tell her to move back in with him and their father, and she didn't want to do that.

"Beak's still back there," he said, inclining his head backward. "He got hung up on the rolling tunnel. He was on the floor as much as he was on his feet. Clowning around, as usual. Sam went back to give him a hand."

"Guy Joe," she said because she was sick of *not* talking about it, "do *you* think the crash was an accident? Tell the truth."

He shrugged. "Who knows? Anything is possible, right? The question is, why would someone do something so awful?"

"Yeah," she agreed solemnly, "that *is* the question." And although her imagination was pretty vivid, she couldn't come up with any reason why someone would commit such a horrible act.

Sam and Beak caught up with them a few minutes later. They took a break, relaxing on the balcony briefly while Beak told a few stupid jokes, and then they all went on together.

The hardest part of the Funhouse for Tess was always the chamber where there was no solid floor, only a cluster of constantly whirling metal saucers. They were slippery, always moving, and there was nothing to grasp for balance except the softly draped black nylon folds on the walls, almost impossible to hold onto, no matter how desperately you clutched. She had discovered long ago that the only way she could make it across was by lowering herself to a sitting position and scooting from saucer to saucer. It took longer, and seriously dented her dignity, but it worked.

She was in the process of doing just that when she realized that she wanted, very much, to go home. She wanted out of this crazy place with its skeletons rattling and its fake bats flying overhead and its dragons breathing foul-smelling smoke in her face. She was tired of feeling like a fool, arms and legs flailing helplessly as she tried to keep her balance on moving boards, linked chains, whirling circles, and rubber tires.

She'd had enough.

Although there were wooden steps exiting the Funhouse in several different places, Tess and her friends always chose the steep metal chute that slid directly to the beach. The walkways were for more timid souls. It was fun to sail down to the beach and land on the sand, legs sprawled every which way.

With a strong sense of relief, Tess did exactly that.

Trudy, Candace, and Gina were already comfortably seated on the beach, watching the waves pounding the shore. Beak, Sam, and Guy Joe followed Tess down the chute.

"Listen, guys," Tess said as she dusted sand from her jeans, "I'm going to split. My head is cracking right down the middle. I need to sleep." Ignoring Gina's protests, she reached into the back pocket of her jeans. And groaned.

"My keys are gone!" she cried in dismay. "I put my key case in my back pocket so I wouldn't have to lug my purse around with me in there," she said, waving toward the Funhouse. "They must have fallen out." She groaned again. "My stomach can't handle that place again, not this soon! It hasn't recovered from that stupid rolling tunnel!"

Gina stood up. "I'll go. I know your key case. The red leather one with your initials on it, right?"

"You'll never find that key case in there," Beak argued. "Get maintenance to look for it."

"Why doesn't Tess go herself?" Trudy asked. "They're *her* keys."

"Why don't we all go?" Sam said as Gina turned to leave. "Tess can show us exactly where she did most of her usual acrobatics so we'll know where the keys would most likely have fallen out of her pocket."

"No, that's silly," Gina said, waving a hand in dismissal. "I'll go, and I'll be right back. I know the Funhouse like the back of my hand and," she added with a grin, "my stomach's cast-iron, everyone knows that." And she turned and ran up the beach.

"Where's she going?" asked Doss, as he joined them.

"To find Tess's car keys," Trudy answered. "She lost them in the Funhouse."

"Then why is *Gina* looking for them?" Doss asked.

"Oh, for heaven's sake!" Tess cried, "I'll go, I'll go!"

The thought of entering the Funhouse again made her sick. But it was true — the keys were hers, she was the one who had lost them, and Gina shouldn't have to look for them alone. She turned to follow her up the beach.

Entering the Funhouse, Tess wondered how they would ever find the key case. The place had so many little nooks and crannies, so many cracks in the wooden floors, and then there were all those open spaces between the whirling circles. The keys might even have fallen through to the beach. If they didn't find the case in here, they'd have to sift through the sand next.

"Gina!" she called as she entered the rolling wooden walkway and clutched at the padded walls. "Gina, wait up!"

She had hurried through the tilting tunnel and was headed for the first of the open balconies, when a sound stopped her in her tracks.

It was a piercing scream that sent slivers of ice sliding down her back.

That scream wasn't a normal part of the Funhouse. It hadn't come from a witch's cackling mouth or a dangling skeleton or a bloody corpse. That scream had been real.

And the voice had been familiar. Very familiar.

Although she didn't want to believe it, the voice had belonged to Gina Giambone.

And it hadn't been an Oh-gosh-I'm-scared Funhouse kind of scream. Tess could recognize a scream of genuine fear when she heard it.

Calling Gina's name, Tess tried desperately to run. But it was impossible, given the footing underneath her as she entered the puffed-pillow passageway. She stumbled and fell several times before reaching solid footing again. Her breath came in ragged gasps, threatening to stick in her throat. Calls to Gina brought only silence in return.

Safer, more solid wooden walkways around each challenge brought her quickly to the chamber of metal saucers. They were separated by small spaces through which glimpses of the beach below could be seen. The spaces were so tiny they provided no danger, as only a toothpick-sized person could slip through and fall to the hard-packed sand below.

Unless . . . unless one of the large round circles was missing.

And one *was*.

Tess stared at the gap in the flooring, her mouth open, eyes wide as she realized that she could see, quite clearly, to the beach below. She could see the tan sand, flat in some spots, mounded into little hillocks by the wind in other places. She could see a small green plastic pail left by a careless child. And she could see . . . Gina.

She was lying on the sand, her left leg sticking out at a sickening angle, her face, in profile, twisted in agony.

And she was lying very, very still.

Chapter 11

Stupid Gina! Getting in the way like that. If it hadn't been for her goody-two-shoes helpfulness, it would have been Tess who fell through the hole, just as I'd planned. Slipping the key case out of her back pocket was a cinch, and the plan would have worked perfectly, if it hadn't been for Tess's weak stomach and Gina's Girl Scout instincts.

It was Tess's fault more than Gina's. The keys belonged to Tess. And that hole was designed for her. She really screwed up my schedule. She'll have to pay for that. I can't let people get away with fouling things up for me. I'll have to think of something special for her. To punish her.

Like I wish I could punish that Buddy in Lila's journal.

Buddy came to see me today. He says he knows a wonderful family who will give my baby a good home when it's born. I couldn't believe it! Does he think that just because Tully is gone, I would give away our child? I threw him out.

The next entry was several days later.

Buddy keeps pressuring me to give up my baby. He comes back every day, saying I'll never get a job on The Boardwalk because the new owners don't want me there. They think I'll make the customers uncomfortable after what Tully did right there in the Funhouse. He says I'll never be able to earn a living and support my baby. And then he said his friends, who want a child more than anything, could give my baby everything.

He keeps saying that if I really cared about my baby I'd give it up. What am I going to do?

A few days later:

Buddy was back again today. He told me this family that wants my baby has offered to pay my rent and my expenses until the baby's born. The only strings attached, he says, are that they get the baby when it's born, and I don't let anyone know that I'm pregnant. When I asked him why, he said, "My friends wouldn't want anyone to know the baby isn't theirs. The woman has gone to Europe and expects to be given the child when she returns, and she'll tell everyone she had the baby in England."

I have to let him help me now. I have no choice. I have so little money left, and no one will give me a job. So I'll have to accept their money for now, for my baby. But I'll think of something before the baby's born. I'm not going to give up my baby.

Chapter 12

Tess's only thought as she struggled through the remaining passageways toward an exit was, No, not Gina. Not Gina! Fake bats swung down from the ceiling, diving for her head. Dragons on the walls breathed hot smoke in her face. Skeletons rattled their bones in a crazy dance. She brushed them all aside and kept going. Don't be dead, Gina, she prayed. Don't be dead like Dade Lewis!

What would she ever do without Gina?

Gina wasn't dead. But she was unconscious. Tess's companions had already gathered around her limp body. Beak was kneeling by her side, holding one of her hands, with Doss on the other side. Beachgoers gathered around the small group as the sun sank beneath the sea.

"Someone call an ambulance," Beak cried as Tess, gasping for breath, her face tear-streaked, arrived and knelt at Gina's side. Someone called, "I'll go," and Beak turned back to Gina, calling her name repeatedly.

She didn't answer.

There didn't seem to be any blood. But Tess hated the fact that the big dark eyes refused to open. The smoothly packed sand was almost as hard as wood, and Gina had fallen a long way.

Jim Mancini, The Boardwalk's manager, pushed through the growing crowd. A short, squat man wearing tan pants and a white shirt with the sleeves rolled up to the elbow, he made a soft sound when he saw Gina lying on the sand. "What happened?" he asked as he knelt beside her and lifted her wrist to check her pulse. "She's alive," he said. A murmur of relief rose from the crowd. Turning toward Tess, he asked, "Did she hit her head? How long has she been unconscious? What's wrong with her leg?"

There was definitely something wrong with Gina's leg. No normal bone could make such a crazy angle.

"It's broken," volunteered Sam, whose father was a doctor. "Fractured, probably. Doesn't look like a clean break."

"I don't understand how this happened," Tess said in a bewildered voice over the sound of an approaching siren. "Why was that circle missing?"

Mancini's eyes narrowed. "Missing? What was missing?"

With tears in her eyes, Tess answered, "One of the spinning circles in the Funhouse. It was . . . gone. It had been there when we went through earlier. But this time, when I followed Gina into that passageway to see why she had screamed, one of the circles was gone. There was just this great big hole. Gina probably didn't see it in time and fell right through."

Mancini would have questioned her further, but the ambulance arrived just then. Tess wanted to ride in it with Gina, but the paramedics discouraged her.

"Call her parents," one of them said, "and have them meet us at the Medical Center." As he turned away to help carry the stretcher, he told his colleague, "I was on duty the other night when that roller coaster went. Some mess! And now this! I'm keeping my kids away from here from now on."

Tess turned away, intent on going straight to her car and then to the Medical Center. She wanted to be with Gina.

But Mancini stopped her. "Look," he said, "your friend's in good hands. You can see her later. Right now, I need you to show me where this happened. So it won't happen to somebody else."

Tess realized he had a point. That missing circle was dangerous. And she probably wouldn't be allowed to see Gina for a while, anyway.

She nodded. "Okay, come on. But I need to call Gina's parents first." She bit her lip anxiously. "They're going to be so upset."

"Someone already called," Candace said softly, putting a sympathetic arm around Tess's shoulders. "I heard someone say so."

"Good!" Mancini said. "Then we can get right to it. Come on, miss, show me what you were talking about."

Which Tess would have been happy to do, except for one thing. When she led Mancini and her friends into the chamber, there was absolutely nothing to see.

Because not a single circle was missing.

Tess stared at the spot where the gaping hole had been. It was now filled by a whirling, innocent-looking saucer, just as it was supposed to be. The disk stared right back at her as if to say, "But I've been here all along. You were imagining things!"

She could feel everyone's eyes on her after they'd searched in vain for anything out of the ordinary. "I don't believe this," she said slowly, feeling a flush rise up out of her neck and spread to her face.

"Well, *I* don't get it!" Mancini said, eyeing Tess suspiciously. "There's nothing wrong here. What were you talking about down on the beach?"

"It was gone!" she cried. "It was!" She knew, even as she said it, how crazy that sounded. After all, the circles were huge. Someone couldn't just lift one out and walk away with it without being seen. "The one in the middle was missing. There was a hole there! That's how I could see Gina, lying on the beach."

No one said a word. And that silence told her, very clearly, that no one believed her.

"Honestly, Tess," Trudy said lazily, "first you see some dark spirit under The Devil's Elbow and now you're seeing missing saucers. I thought people like you always saw *flying* saucers."

And even though Candace said, "Trudy, don't be so mean!" and Sam moved closer to Tess and said,

"Take it easy, Tess. You're upset about Gina," Tess began to shake violently. Her arms and legs trembled and Sam had to take hold of her with both hands to keep her upright.

"I know what I saw," Tess managed to say. "And if I didn't see it, then exactly how *did* Gina end up on the beach?"

Mancini shrugged toward the passageway up ahead. "Tumbled over the railing, maybe."

The railing was high, to protect small children from accidental falls. And Gina wasn't clumsy. "She couldn't have fallen over that railing," Tess argued. "It's too high."

"I think you'd better talk to the police, miss," he said coolly. "Something fishy here. I had my assistant give them a call. They should be here by now. You were the only person in here when your friend fell. They'll want to talk to you."

The police? A chilly fog descended upon Tess. "But I want to go to the Medical Center," she argued as they all left the Funhouse, taking the wooden stairs.

"That will have to wait," the manager said sternly, taking her elbow as they reached the foot of the stairs. Dusk had fallen and the air had turned chilly. Tess shivered. But she wasn't really cold. She was frightened. "We need to clear this up right now. I don't want any questions," Mancini went on, "about The Boardwalk's safety."

"Too late," Sam said drily. "Two accidents in one week makes for a lot of questions."

Ignoring his remark, Mancini gripped the sleeve

of Tess's yellow sweatshirt and led her to his office. Her friends followed, grumbling their support for her to themselves. Candace looked even more pale and frightened than usual, and Guy Joe's lips were drawn together tightly in anger. Tess could feel people along The Boardwalk staring at them, and knew that by nightfall the story of Tess Landers being dragged into Mancini's office would be all over town. Her face felt feverish, and she kept her eyes on the ground.

The police questioning wasn't as bad as she'd feared. There were only two uniformed men and they were more polite than Mancini had been. They asked her to take them back to the Funhouse and point out the spot where Gina had fallen. When they could find no evidence of any circle having been tampered with, they walked away from her, talking in low voices. But Tess heard every word.

"Isn't this the girl who brought that note in?" the taller one asked his partner. "You know, the one in purple crayon that Boz showed us?"

Boz. The desk sergeant, Tess guessed, and her cheeks burned with humiliation as the second policeman answered, "Yeah. One of those rich kids, lives up on the hill. Broken home and all that. Probably gets everything at home except attention, know what I mean?" He shook his head sadly.

She couldn't just let them dismiss her as some kind of attention-getting kook. "Excuse me," she said politely.

They turned around.

"If the saucer really wasn't missing," she asked

them, "how could Gina have fallen? There isn't any place here for her to fall through to the beach. Not with all the saucers in place."

"Good question," the tall policeman said heartily. "And you have our word, miss, that the matter will be investigated thoroughly. We may have to call on you again."

They wouldn't call on her again, and she knew it. But she also knew there wasn't any way to convince them that she was telling the truth. She had no proof.

"Look, kid," the taller policeman said, "you can go collect your friends now. We'll look into this, I promise. You're probably anxious to find out how your friend is."

He was being nice. Trying to smile, she admitted that she was anxious to get to the Medical Center. Now if only Gina was fine.

Gina wasn't fine. And they weren't allowed to see her, Tess was informed by the emergency room nurse. "You can wait in there," she said crisply, pointing toward a room at the end of the hall. Tess, seeing Mr. Giambone pacing the hall outside of the waiting room, ran to see if Gina's parents knew anything about her condition.

They didn't. No one had told them anything.

The sight of Gina's normally cheerful mother weeping, her hands over her face, shocked Tess. She wanted to say something to comfort the woman who had always been so good to her, but nothing seemed right. Quietly, Tess took a seat beside her.

"The doctor said she'd be in there a while," Doss

said, his usual swaggering air gone as he gestured toward the emergency room. He seemed as worried as everyone else in the room.

But suspicion had taken a firm hold on Tess and was growing with every passing minute. Two accidents in less than a week! In a town where things like this never happened. She didn't care *what* explanation for Gina's fall the police came up with, they'd never convince her that the saucer hadn't been missing. It *had*. Someone had taken it. She didn't have the slightest idea *how* someone would do such a thing. She only knew that someone had.

But who?

The person who had written the purple note, of course. The intention was clear from that awful poem. The police, and then Gina, hadn't taken it seriously. Maybe they should have. If there'd been no more accidents, Tess would have agreed with them that it was just a sick joke. But now Gina had fallen, and it was clear, at least to *Tess*, that the note had been for real.

What frightened Tess most was the fact that every single person who had been *seriously* hurt so far, with the exception of some innocent bystanders injured in The Devil's Elbow crash, had been her age, in her group of friends: Dade, Sheree, Joey, and now Gina. Why would someone target them?

And then Tess thought of something else, even more frightening.

Whoever had slipped that purple note under her door had known where she lived — that she lived with Shelley in the condominium, not with her father anymore. Only a few people knew that. Only her closest friends.

But that was impossible! None of her friends could ever do anything this horrible. Never! Could they?

Tess glanced around the room nervously. Could shy, quiet Candace be harboring feelings of hatred and anger toward her fellow students? Why? Because she felt left out? If people didn't pay that much attention to Candace, it was because she was so quiet. Maybe underneath that quiet, she was full of rage. Maybe she wasn't who they all thought she was.

Beak? Lover of practical jokes? Even he couldn't possibly find The Devil's Elbow crash funny — could he?

Trudy? Remembering the temper tantrum that Trudy had thrown in the school parking lot, Tess watched Trudy for a long moment. Wearing an expensive pink jumpsuit belted in rich leather, Trudy was filing her nails with an emery board, glancing up every now and then to smile at Guy Joe, who lounged against the wall. Could Trudy have some reason for wanting the people she knew well to suffer?

I can't believe, Tess thought unhappily, that I am even considering the possibility that one of my friends could have done such horrid things! It's just not possible, that's all!

Then who had? And why?

Doss, she thought, as she looked across the room at him, slumped in one of the hard plastic chairs.

Doss would know the Funhouse inside and out. And he'd know how to remove those metal saucers and replace them, wouldn't he?

The trouble with that theory, she realized instantly, was that Gina would be the last person Doss would want to hurt. Anyone who had seen the expression on his square, dark face when he looked at Gina would understand that Doss would rather break his *own* leg than Gina's.

That was when she remembered something, and sat up straight. Of course! The missing saucer hadn't been intended for Gina. The missing keys belonged to *Tess*. The hole in the saucers had been created for *her*. And those keys hadn't slid from her pocket at all. They'd been deliberately removed. That's why she hadn't been able to find them anywhere, and had to get a lift back home to pick up her extra set.

But who would have had the opportunity to take her keys? Doss would have. She now remembered he had been standing close to her on The Boardwalk before they'd first entered the Funhouse. He could easily have filched her keys. And then he could have removed the saucer, knowing Tess would return to the Funhouse to search for them.

But how on earth would someone time a stunt like that? And where would they put the missing saucer? There wasn't any place in the passageway to hide something so large.

Never mind. She'd figure all of that out later. Right now, it was enough to realize that Gina's fall hadn't been an accident, that it hadn't been intended for Gina, and that the note had been perfectly serious when it said *Who will be next?*

Tess shivered in her seat.

"Cold?" Sam asked, coming up to stand in front of her. "Want my jacket?" He slipped out of his brown suede jacket and handed it to her, but she shook her head no.

"Not cold," she said quietly. "Just thinking ugly thoughts."

He sat down beside her. "Like?"

She wasn't ready to share what she'd been thinking. Saying it aloud would make it so much more real. She had to do some more heavy thinking before she told anyone.

"Never mind."

He accepted that, and sat quietly beside her, asking no more questions.

"This is such a bad thing," Mrs. Giambone said suddenly. "My Gina, she was in such pain when they brought her in."

"She was conscious? That's a good sign, isn't it?"

The woman nodded, her round face, so like Gina's, creased with worry. "She was awake. But she was crying. And I cried, too." She shook her head, her curly graying hair moving with the motion. "That's not good, for a mother to cry in front of her child. It scared my Gina. But I couldn't help it."

Tess put an arm around Mrs. Giambone's ample shoulders. "She'll be okay. Honest, she will." Because anything else was unthinkable. "And I don't blame you for crying. I cried, too, when I saw her on the beach."

Until she saw Mrs. Giambone weeping, Tess hadn't given a thought to what all of this must be like for the parents. Sheree Buchanan's mother had spent most of Sheree's life bragging about how pretty her daughter was. Joey's parents came to every single track meet, even the out-of-town events. And the Giambones were understandably scared to death.

It's worse for them, Tess thought with conviction. It's worse for the parents.

Her head began to pound furiously. The words *Who will be next?* danced across the white walls, taunting her. *Who will be next, who will be —*

Dr. Oliver, Sam's father, stethoscope around his neck, appeared in the doorway. Mr. Giambone was right behind him.

"Your daughter," the doctor told the parents, "has a fractured leg and a mild concussion. We're going to keep her here for a while. No visitors for a day or two. Except, of course, for you two. You can go in and see her now, before we take her upstairs. She's worried about you."

"We can't see her?" Tess asked, her voice quivering slightly. She wouldn't be certain Gina was okay until she saw that for herself.

Dr. Oliver shook his head. "Sorry. Not yet. Give her some time to get over the shock to her system. A good night's sleep is what she needs right now.

Maybe tomorrow, although the next day would be even better, okay?"

It wasn't okay. But she had to do what was best for Gina. Because in a way, this was all *her* fault. It had been her key case. The hole had been meant for her. So the fall, the concussion, and the fractured leg should have been hers, too.

Perhaps because of her guilt, Tess stayed for a while after everyone else went home, hoping Sam's father would change his mind and let her see Gina.

He didn't, and when she was so tired she felt like she was about to collapse, she left, too.

She hurried to her car, hating the darkness and wishing she had asked someone to wait with her. But who? Right now, she was so unsure about everyone she knew that she couldn't think of a single person she absolutely trusted.

She cried quietly all the way home. Last night she had been safe in the Giambone house, drinking hot coffee and eating homemade doughnuts with a sugar glaze, fresh from Mrs. Giambone's deep fryer. She'd been sitting at the big wooden table in the warm, friendly kitchen, surrounded by large and small Giambones and laughing at the antics of the littlest ones.

Laughing. She'd been laughing! Had that been last night? It seemed like a million years ago.

At The Shadows, she parked the car, jumped out, locked the car doors, and was about to race for the kitchen door when something caught her eye.

There was an object hanging from the black

wrought-iron top of the light fixture on the wall beside the kitchen door. She'd forgotten to turn on the light before she left, so she couldn't see very clearly.

Peering into the shadows, she moved a step closer. The object was white. Not white-white, but grayish-white. A bundle of something? Paper? Rags? What would a bundle of paper or rags be doing on her light fixture?

She took another step closer. It looked soft and furry, like her angora sweater. White and soft and furry? What was white and soft and furry?

Scarcely breathing, Tess moved one more step closer to the light fixture. A sudden breeze sent the object swaying back and forth. Glassy blue eyes turned in the breeze, staring at her coldly.

Trilby.

Tess screamed.

Chapter 13

Poor Tess. What a fright that pretty kitty gave her.

I was in the attic so long that day, that it grew dark. I didn't even realize it until I could no longer read Lila O'Hare's faint scrawl. I pulled the chain on the bulb hanging from the ceiling. I wasn't about to leave until I'd finished the journal. It just got more and more interesting.

Buddy was taking care of her financial needs. He certainly owed her that much, after taking everything she owned. And still that wasn't enough for him. He wanted more. He wanted her child.

Buddy won't tell me who the people are who want my baby. But I think I know. And if it's who I think it is, they certainly could give my baby everything money can buy. And I do worry about that. Maybe I'm being selfish, not considering an adoption that could give my child the best life possible. I know I can't give it to him or her. Buddy says a good mother would care more for her child's happiness than she does her own. Maybe he's right.

Chapter 14

As Tess continued screaming, lights began glowing in first one unit, then another. Doors opened and heads peeked out, turning toward her screams. But no one ventured forth.

A car door slammed behind her. Footsteps hurried across the cement patio toward her. Hands grabbed her shoulders, shook her, repeatedly saying her name.

"Tess! Tess, it's Guy Joe! What on earth is wrong?"

Her brother was standing in front of her, blocking her view of the light fixture and the grisly thing hanging from it. He was flanked on one side by Sam and Trudy, on the other by a white-faced Candace. They were all wearing matching blue Santa Luisa High windbreakers, except Candace, shrouded in a faded tan raincoat and matching hat.

With the swaying animal blocked from her vision, Tess was able to catch her breath. But she couldn't speak. Instead, she pointed a shaking finger past Guy Joe.

Sam moved forward in the direction of the pointed finger. Tess watched in dread as he moved closer to the door. Tilting his head, he examined the object of Tess's terror.

After a moment, he called over his shoulder, "It's not real."

"What?" Tess whispered, sagging against Guy Joe.

"It's not real," Sam repeated. "It's stuffed. It's a stuffed animal, like the kind Candace has overpopulating her bedroom." He reached up and yanked the pile of fluff loose from the cord holding it suspended in the air. Then he returned to Tess, the freed object in his hands. "It's not real, Tess. See for yourself."

"Stuffed?" Tess said softly. "It's stuffed?"

Sam held it in his outstretched hands. "Does look real, though, doesn't it?"

Tess took the soft, fluffy creature in her own hands and turned it over repeatedly, murmuring, "It's not Trilby, it's not Trilby." When she was finally satisfied that it really was not Gina's cat, she let it slip to the patio and began crying quietly.

"Trilby?" Trudy said, taking a seat in a white patio chair. "What's a Trilby?"

"Gina's cat," Tess said quietly, sinking into a chair opposite Trudy because it suddenly occurred to her that if she didn't sit down, she would fall down. "You know, the big Siamese. She looks exactly like . . . that," pointing toward the object lying on the patio stone.

Trudy frowned. "Why would Gina's cat be hanging from your lamppost? Honestly, Tess, you just get weirder and weirder!"

Candace came up behind Tess and put both hands on Tess's shoulders. "Shut up, Trudy," she said firmly, surprising all of them. "How could Tess know why it was there? The point is, it was, and it must have been a horrible thing for her. Leave her alone."

And Guy Joe, taking a seat beside Trudy, said, "I don't know about you, Trudy. Sometimes you scare me. You must have ice water in your veins. Ever hear of the word *compassion*?"

Trudy pouted.

Sam sat down in the chair next to Tess's, and took one of her hands in his. "It wasn't real, Tess." "I know it must have looked it, but it wasn't," he said softly. "It's a good thing we decided to drop by tonight."

Guy Joe took a book of matches lying on the round white table and lit a short, stubby citronella candle sitting in a glass dish in the table's center. Tess watched as the resulting light cast an eerie glow over the faces looking at her. Or was she imagining the eerieness? Was she so spooked now that everything and everyone seemed sinister to her?

Well, why shouldn't she be? Wouldn't anyone be, if the same cruel joke had been played on them?

"So Gina loaned you her cat," Trudy said, scooting her chair closer to Guy Joe's. "That still doesn't explain why you thought it would be hanging from your light fixture."

"I didn't *think* it was, Trudy!" Tess said hotly.

"It was! Or, at least, something that looked exactly like Trilby. And I have no idea why someone would pull such a rotten stunt. I also don't know why someone would deliberately sabotage The Devil's Elbow, or remove one of the saucers from the Funhouse or write me a threatening note."

"You got a threatening note?" Guy Joe and Sam said in one voice. And Sam added, "Why didn't you tell me?"

She didn't mention that they'd hardly been on speaking terms. This was not the time. "I didn't tell anyone," she said bitterly, "because so far no one has believed anything I've said about any of this stuff. Everyone says the crash was an accident, and that the saucer wasn't missing even though I saw it with my own eyes, and the police practically laughed me out of the station when I took my note in for them to see. So why would I tell anyone else about it?"

"What did it say?" Guy Joe wanted to know.

She told them. She knew the words by heart and would never forget them.

"Oh, Tess," Candace breathed when Tess had finished reciting the purple words, "that's awful! You must have been so scared! I would have been."

"Of course you would have," Trudy said cruelly, "you're afraid of your own shadow. And you wouldn't have the sense to realize that it was just a big, fat joke. But I'm sure Tess does, don't you, Tess?"

"It doesn't sound like a joke to me," Guy Joe said grimly. "Tess, I think you should move back to the house with Dad and me. At least until good old Shelley comes back. Not that she'd be much protection," he added coldly, "but at least you wouldn't be alone. How about it? Come home with me tonight?"

"That's the best idea I've heard," Sam agreed. "Even if it is a joke, you shouldn't be alone after the shock you just had."

The idea was tempting. Her father's house was solid brick, with an iron gate around the huge property. How could she not be safe there? It would be so easy to just leave the condo and go stay where people could take care of her.

No. She'd always done that. And her father wouldn't "take care" of her. He'd take charge of her. The two things weren't the same at all. She didn't want to take any stupid, foolish chances, but she didn't want to go running home to daddy, either, especially since "daddy" hadn't once called or come to see her since Shelley and Tess had left the house.

"No," she said as firmly as she could manage. "I don't think so. Not tonight. I need to think, and I can do that better here, in my own house."

"I'll stay with you, Tess," Candace said quietly, "if you want me to."

Tess was deeply touched. Trudy had been right earlier: Candace *was* a little like a scared rabbit. To offer her company in a house that might not be one hundred percent safe was a sweet thing to do. It must have taken great effort on Candace's part. Refusing her offer might hurt her feelings. Besides, she would hardly get in the way. Most of the time, people weren't even aware that Candace was around. And while Tess may have been confused about other things, she was sure that there was no way Candace could have had any part in the awful things that had happened. No question there. And it *would* be nice to have some company.

"Thank you, Candace," Tess said, "that would be nice."

"Oh, great!" Sam complained, "now I not only have to worry about you, I have to worry about my sister, too. That's just perfect!"

He was going to worry about her? What about their heated argument when he had said he was washing his hands of her for good? Washing your hands of someone for good didn't include worrying about them, did it?

"We'll be fine," she reassured him. "I'll lock all the doors and windows and put my attack cat in the window. Quit worrying."

She stood up, ignoring the annoyed look on Sam's face. "Now you guys, go home. I've never been so tired in my life! I'm going to bed." She managed a slight grin. "Sam, if you're so worried, you can sleep in a chair out here. I'll even bring you a blanket."

For just a minute or so, she thought he might actually accept. And she wouldn't have minded. It might have been nice, falling asleep knowing he was out there.

"No way," he said angrily. "I'm not freezing my buns off just because you're too stubborn to go back to your dad's. Find some other knight in shining armor. This one's going home to his own nice, warm bed."

"Chivalry is dead," Trudy said gaily, standing up and taking Guy Joe's hand. "Well, Tess, you had your chance to return to the castle where you'd be protected by the moat. If anything terrible happens to you, it's your own fault."

Is that a threat? Tess wondered, and was amazed by the thought. Trudy? Well, why not? She could have tied the cat on the light fixture earlier. Could have written the poem, too. As for the missing saucer, well, Trudy the athlete and ballet dancer was certainly strong and agile enough to handle that.

But the question of motive remained unanswered.

When they had gone, Tess and Candace went inside. The first thing Tess did was flip on every available light switch. The second thing she did was scoop Trilby up out of her wicker basket and sit stroking the soft, very much alive body until her own nerves settled down. Then she showed Candace where everything was, lent her a pair of pajamas, and gave Candace her own bed, explaining that she wouldn't be using it. She intended to take up her vigilant position on the couch, poker at her side, after making sure that every door and window in the place was locked and the oval table was still firmly pressed against the French doors.

When she finally settled down under the afghan, Trilby was already fast asleep on the couch.

Tess wasn't so lucky. In spite of her emotional

and physical exhaustion, she had a hard time turning off the turmoil in her mind so that she could sleep. Her best friend was in the hospital, the result of tampering aimed at Tess, someone had played a terribly cruel joke on *her* tonight, and what was worst of all, she knew this wasn't the end of it. There was more to come; she could feel it.

What next? she wondered fearfully just before she fell asleep.

She was awakened some time in the middle of the night, by the shrilling of the telephone on the lamp table behind her head. Struggling to wake up, she thought: Shelley. She'd forgotten or ignored the time difference. Typical Shelley.

Swivelling awkwardly, she reached to pick up the phone. It wasn't Shelley.

"It's your fault Gina's in the hospital," a voice she didn't recognize whispered in her ear. "You messed everything up. You'll have to be punished for that. Soon. Very soon."

Tess struggled upward on the couch, trying to comprehend the whispered words.

"Did you like my present tonight?" the horrid voice continued.

"Who is this?" she cried, knowing she wouldn't get an answer.

"Meow!" the voice said, and hung up.

Chapter 15

All I have to do is wait. That's what Lila O'Hare did. She waited, all those months, for her baby, and for Buddy to stop pressuring her to sign the adoption papers. She waited for someone to come to her rescue.

No one did.

And being alone took its toll on her; I could tell from the way her writing changed. As the journal went on she seemed more and more tired and hopeless. Buddy's badgering was really getting to her.

The question that had been nagging at me ever since I'd started reading the journal was still unanswered: Who was this Buddy? Was he still alive and living in Santa Luisa?

And even more important: What was this journal doing in my house?

Chapter 16

Tess awoke the next day, bleary-eyed from lack of sleep, to find that the rainy season had begun. Slate-gray skies overhead promised a steady downpour throughout the day.

And like the weather, the atmosphere inside Santa Luisa High School was grim. A sudden, painful acquaintance with multiple tragedies had affected every student and teacher. Even the usually raucous students walked the halls with heads down, talking in hushed voices.

"Doesn't anyone," Tess asked at lunch, "think two accidents in less than a week is a little suspicious? Has anyone heard anything from Chalmers? He should know something about The Devil's Elbow crash by now." She didn't mention her phone call of the night before. While it had terrified her, in broad daylight, it seemed a little fuzzy, and she wasn't sure that it hadn't been a dream. She had a feeling her friends wouldn't be convinced, either. She would keep the phone call to herself, for now.

"I heard it was a loose rail," Beak said casually

as he sectioned an orange, looping the peel around the wrist of Trudy, who sat beside him.

Trudy chose to ignore him, focusing all of her attention on Guy Joe, sitting opposite her, beside Tess. "My dad said at breakfast this morning that Chalmers told him the rail would be fixed, and an accident like that wouldn't happen again for at least another hundred years. A freak thing, he said."

"A loose rail? That's it? A loose rail?" Tess shook her head and sank back in her chair. "Are we supposed to buy that?"

"Tess," Beak warned, "you'd better lighten up or you'll lose it totally. Don't let this stuff get to you, okay? It's probably all coincidence, anyway. No dire plot, no sinister doings, just coincidence. Stuff happens, you know?"

"Leave Tess alone," Sam said lazily, dousing his hard-boiled egg with salt. "She had a rough day yesterday."

"We all did, Sam," Trudy reminded him sharply. "And I don't want to talk about this gloomy stuff anymore. I'm sick of it. And I am *having* my birthday party Saturday night, on the beach, the way I planned. You'd all better be there, or I'll never speak to a single one of you ever again!" A coquettish smile accompanied that threat.

"Promises, promises," Tess murmured. Aloud, she said, "Party? You're having a party? Now?"

Trudy tossed her thick, blonde hair. A fat pink velvet bow sat atop it, matching her short-sleeved sweater. "Yes, Tess, I'm funny that way. I like to celebrate my birthday on the day I was born."

"On the day you were born," Beak said with a grin, "your parents wouldn't give you permission for a party."

"Very funny, Beak. I mean, on the anniversary of the day I was born. Quit trying so hard to be cute."

"Oh, it's no effort. Comes naturally. You really having a party this Saturday?"

"What is the *matter* with you people? Don't you understand plain English? I just said I was, didn't I?"

"Holding a party at The Boardwalk," Tess said, toying with her sandwich, which remained untouched in its wrapper, "is like holding a party on a runway at a busy airport! You're just asking for trouble, Trudy. Haven't you been paying attention? People have been getting hurt over there."

Trudy's blue eyes narrowed. "Is that a threat, Tess? You were around both times something awful happened at The Boardwalk. That's a pretty major coincidence, don't you think?"

Tess gasped. "That isn't funny, Trudy! How could you even think such a thing?"

"Cut it out, Trudy," Sam warned. "Tess didn't have anything to do with that stuff, and you know it."

"Shame on you, Trudy," Candace scolded, her ponytail bouncing with the unusual vigor of her words, "Tess would never, ever hurt anyone!"

Unperturbed, Trudy shrugged. "All I know," she said stubbornly, "is that Tess was the only other person in the Funhouse when Gina fell."

That was too much for Tess. For all she knew, Trudy wasn't the only person in school who felt that way. People had been staring at her all day. She'd thought it was because she looked like such a wreck, but now she wasn't so sure.

"Ignore her," Candace said softly. "She's just being mean."

But as comforting as the words were, they weren't enough. Tess, biting her lip fiercely to keep herself from bursting into tears, stood up and hurried away from the table and out of the cafeteria. She was conscious of stares and whispers following her every step of the way.

Fury fueled her steps. Wasn't it enough that someone was torturing her with menacing notes and phone calls? Wasn't it enough that she was alone out there in the condo, without anyone around who cared about her? Wasn't it enough that her best friend was lying flat on her back in a hospital bed? People like Trudy had no right suspecting her. No right at all!

Quit feeling sorry for yourself, she scolded herself. At least you're walking on your own two feet, which is more than you can say for Gina.

After school, Tess went straight to the Medical Center, the heavy rain forcing her to drive slowly. On the way there, she passed The Boardwalk. It was almost deserted, with only a handful of cars in the huge parking lot. That couldn't be because of the weather, she told herself, since most of the amusement park was covered. If anything, The

Boardwalk was usually busier in bad weather, since it was one of the few places in town where kids could have fun without braving the elements.

Maybe the thing Mr. Giambone had feared was actually happening. Were people afraid to go near The Boardwalk now, after two serious accidents?

It was at that moment, as she turned a corner toward the Medical Center, that a new thought occurred to her. Maybe . . . maybe people being hurt wasn't the point at all. Maybe the actual target was The Boardwalk itself! The amusement park was hurting for business. Could that have been the goal all along? To cripple The Boardwalk? Or . . . could the target be the board of directors? Dade, Joey, Sheree, and Gina all had something else in common besides being students at Santa Luisa High School. Their parents were all on the board of directors that ran The Boardwalk. And so was her father.

There were eight people on the board. Well, actually only seven since Doss Beecham's father had been forced to resign. So far, four of them had received chilling phone calls summoning them to the Medical Center. Were the others soon to follow?

Pulling into a parking place on the street, she turned off the car's engine and sat quietly behind the wheel, watching the rain slide down her windshield. Should she go to the police with these new theories? On what basis? She had no proof, no new evidence to show them. They were just guesses. They made sense, but she was still missing the one ingredient necessary to clinch her argument: a motive. She had absolutely no idea why someone would want to sabotage The Boardwalk. A disgruntled employee, maybe, seeking revenge? Someone who felt he'd been unfairly fired? How could she find out if there was someone like that?

The best place to seek out that kind of information would be, of course, from one of the members of the board. Like . . . like her father.

She would have to think about that.

Something else occurred to her. Gina! When Gina awakened, she would tell Chief Chalmers and everyone else that the saucer had indeed been missing. Then Chalmers would believe Tess, not only about the saucer, but about the note and the telephone call as well. He'd be convinced, then, that nothing had been accidental. He would know, as she did, that someone in Santa Luisa was deliberately doing these terrible things, and he'd finally do something to stop it.

Gina was the key right now. Because she could also tell Tess who else knew that Tess had taken Trilby home. Only one of *those* people would have hung the stuffed animal from the light fixture. And they had probably done the other horrible things, too. Excited by the possibility of Gina providing answers, Tess hurried into the Medical Center, not even noticing the pelting rain. Now if she could just talk Dr. Oliver into letting her see his patient.

And she did. Gina's head was swathed in white gauze, tiny ringlets of dark hair escaping around the edges. Her cheeks were pale and gray, and her leg was held captive in the air by a torturous-looking pulley arrangement.

Relieved just to see her friend, Tess took a seat on a hard wooden chair beside Gina's bed and took off her jacket. When she had made sure Gina was feeling better, Tess leaned forward slightly, anxious for some answers. "Gina, have you thought at all about how someone might have removed that saucer?"

Gina looked blank. "Saucer? What saucer?"

Tess's heart sank. *Oh, no.* But she persisted. "You know. The one that was missing in the Funhouse. Someone took it out and left a hole. That's what you fell through."

Gina shifted uncomfortably in the bed. "Oh, gee, Tess, didn't the doctor tell you? I don't remember a single thing about yesterday. Not a minute of it! I don't even remember going to the Funhouse. My mom says that's where I got hurt, but it's all a big blank to me. Does it matter? You look awfully worried. What's going on?"

Tess sank back in her chair, crushed with disappointment. Gina had been her only hope. Everything would have been so simple if only Gina had remembered seeing the missing saucer.

"I guess," she said slowly, "that means you don't remember if you told anyone I was taking Trilby home with me, right?"

Gina nodded gingerly. "I didn't even remember that you had," she admitted. "How is she?"

Well, she's not hanging from the light fixture, Tess almost said. But didn't. Because she realized she couldn't tell Gina any of the frightening things that had happened. Not now. Not until she was out of that bed and back in her own home again. Gina had enough to worry about. "She's fine. She's good company. Can I keep her until you get back home?"

"Sure. She probably loves all the attention. She doesn't get much at our house. Too much competition."

In spite of her depression and disappointment, Tess laughed, and changed the subject to a safer topic. They were discussing their teacher Mr. Dart's habit of teasing Gina, when Guy Joe arrived with Beak and Sam. Trudy and Candace walked in a few minutes later. All were soaked, their hair and clothes dripping.

"You all look like drowned rats," Gina said with a smile. "And how did you get in here? The rule is no more than two visitors at a time." Her dark eyes registered disappointment, Tess noticed, when she realized Doss wasn't with them. "If Nurse Nasty finds you in here, you'll be sorry. I swear that woman chuckles with glee every time she gives me a shot. She must have majored in torture tactics instead of nursing."

While they all joked about the nurse, Tess watched them. Not one of them looked like the sort of cruel person who could even *pretend* to hang a cat.

But what about the absent Doss? He would have had more opportunity than anyone else to cause trouble at The Boardwalk. And he had a motive: he might be bitter that his family had lost all of their money while the others still had theirs. The board of directors had fired Mr. Beecham because of his drinking, and the man had really fallen apart after that. Doss might be angry about that.

Angry enough to take Dade Lewis's life?

Maybe.

Her eyes shifted to Beak. Charming, funny Beak, who had once replaced a kettle of soup in the cafeteria with a pot of glue. Had poured a thick layer of honey into every pair of track shoes worn by his teammates, had tied two dozen aluminum cans to the back of a school bus, and had once come to American history class on stilts.

But the things that had happened on The Boardwalk weren't funny, and not even Beak could possibly think so. If he'd done those things, then he wasn't who she thought he was.

But right now, she wasn't sure who *anybody* was.

A moment later Doss arrived, standing awkwardly in the doorway until Gina called to him. A very tall nurse was standing right behind him, her mouth pursed in disapproval as her eyes surveyed the crowd.

"Oh-oh," Gina whispered loudly, "that's her! Florence Frightingale!"

In less than two seconds, the nurse had cleared the room of all but Doss and Tess, the two people Gina had asked to remain as her "legal" visitors.

"The rest of you am-scray now," the nurse said in a no-nonsense voice. "This is no recreation room. Run along."

They did. But as Beak straightened up after kissing Gina on the cheek, his eyes landed on Doss, standing beside Gina's bed. Tess saw the resentment in that look and wondered if she'd made a mistake dismissing Beak as nothing more than a practical joker. That was clearly anger in his eyes. It was gone almost immediately, but she didn't think she'd forget it quickly.

There was a moment of awkward silence after they'd all left. Then Gina, holding one of Doss's hands in her own, smiled at Tess and said, "You are going to Trudy's party, aren't you?"

"No, I *aren't*," Tess answered. "I'm not going near The Boardwalk. I think the place is cursed."

"Oh, come on, Tess!" Gina tried to sit up in bed but was defeated by the cumbersome pulley. "I want Doss to go and have a good time, and he says he won't unless you're there." Another smile. "He feels more comfortable with you than he does with the other guys."

Well, that was a surprise! Or did Doss really want her there, on The Boardwalk Saturday night, for nasty little reasons of his own?

His olive skin flushed with embarrassment. "Hey," he told Gina lightly, "don't talk about me as if I'm not here, okay? I don't want to go to that party without you, anyway."

"Neither do I," Tess agreed.

"Yeah, I know." Gina smiled up at Doss. "But the thing is, I have this problem." She pointed to her airborne leg. "The doctor says the only way I can leave here by Saturday is if I go without my leg. And I hate to do that. I like this leg." She grinned. "You might even say I'm attached to it."

Her visitors groaned.

"Okay, okay, so I'm no Robin Williams. Listen, I really want you guys to go to that party. Please? I know Trudy's a royal pain sometimes, but it's her birthday. Her parents are busy that night and without us, Trudy won't have any celebration at all. I can't go, but you two can. C'mon. For me?"

"That's not fair!" Tess protested. "You're in the hospital. You're hurt. People have to do what you ask or they'll feel like slime. Can't you ask me something easier, like taking a chem test for you or giving every pet in your house a bath?"

"Sam's going," Gina said slyly.

Tess knew her face was as red as Doss's had been a moment earlier. "Like I said, ask me to do something easier."

But Gina looked so disappointed. Tess reminded herself that Gina wouldn't be in a hospital bed if Tess had gone looking for her own key case. And Tess couldn't very well explain that her reluctance to attend the party was based on fear, without telling Gina about the hanging cat and the phone call. She knew she couldn't do that.

"Okay, okay, I'll go." She glared at Gina with mock anger. "Now I suppose you'll demand that I have a good time. Well, sorry, but that's too much to ask."

"Promise me you'll *try* to have a good time."

"Absolutely not." Tess stood up. She was beginning to feel like a third wheel. "I won't promise that. I'll go, but that's all you're getting from me. See you tomorrow."

Gina and Doss were smiling at each other when Tess left the room.

Maybe they were smiling because they didn't realize that something awful could happen at that party. Well, Gina didn't, anyway. Tess wasn't that sure about Doss. He might very well know that something awful was going to happen. She hoped not. Because Gina was falling for him, that was clear as crystal, and she didn't want to see Gina hurt any more than she already had been.

It was still raining hard, and her car was a block away. With only her blue windbreaker for protection, she was soaked through when she reached the car. She was still using her extra set of car keys on a small gold ring. They were harder to find in her shoulder bag than the larger key case, and she was concentrating on locating them when she stepped in a puddle of chilly water that soaked her feet to the ankles. Looking down in dismay, her eyes were distracted by something far more disturbing.

The left front tire directly opposite her feet was no longer doughnut-shaped. It was as flat as a deflated balloon.

Groaning, Tess's eyes went immediately to the rear tire. It, too, was completely flat.

A feeling of dread rising within her, she sloshed around the rear of the car to the other side. And sagged against the door as her eyes focused on two more thoroughly deflated tires.

One flat tire would have annoyed her, especially in such lousy weather. Two would have surprised her, although she supposed that sort of thing happened sometimes.

But four flat tires was an unmistakable message.

Her breathing was shallow as she bent in the rain to examine first one tire, then the others, more carefully. She found exactly what she had feared she would find.

All four tires had been deliberately slashed.

Chapter 17

Ha, ha, ha. Shredded tires. Now her car won't go!

I think she knows I've been following her. Keeps looking over her shoulder. Reminds me of a deer I saw once when my dad made me go hunting with him. It knew we were after it. I felt sorry for it. But I don't feel sorry for Tess. Why should I?

Lila decided to give up her baby for adoption. I knew it was coming, but it still made me angry when I got to that entry.

I don't know what else to do. I'm so tired. And Buddy's right. I can't provide what a baby needs. I've tried and tried to think of a way, but there is none.

He keeps telling me how much these people want a baby of their own. Doesn't that mean they'll love it and care for it? I hope so.

But anyway, it's too late now. I've signed the adoption papers. I pray I did the right thing . . .

I knew, somehow, that she didn't.

Chapter 18

Staring at the shredded tires on her car didn't make them suddenly inflate, so Tess straightened up and looked around her, her heart thudding in her chest. Someone had done this deliberately.

Sagging against the useless car, her wet hair and clothes clinging to her she thought, Gina had a lot of visitors tonight. Every single one of them knows this is my car. Someone I know — one of my friends — is after me and I have no idea why. The thought made Tess feel sick. She heard the whisper again. *"You'll have to be punished . . . soon."*

What should she do now? Call the police? She'd have to tell them who she suspected, the whole long list of names. She couldn't do that. She had no proof. They'd never believe that any child of one of The Boardwalk's directors, the most powerful people in town, was responsible for all the turmoil.

Which child *was* it?

And why were they hurting people in Santa Luisa?

She was stranded. How was she going to get

home? Any minute now, Doss Beecham would leave the hospital and find Tess stranded out here. Although she wasn't *sure* he was the one, that thought made her more nervous than the slashed tires. All she knew was that she wanted to get home, out of the rain, where she could think straight.

Turning, she hurried away from the car and out into the road leading up the hill toward The Shadows.

Halfway up the hill, misery overtook her with full force. She was alone in the dark and the wind and the rain and she was frightened. Where was the tire-slasher now?

Was he watching her? Tess glanced around nervously. The hill and the woods on either side seemed deserted. But were they? Wouldn't the sound of footsteps be muffled by the wind and the rain?

Realizing just how vulnerable she was, walking out in the open up the main road, she decided it would be safer to take a shortcut through the woods. It would be muddier, and therefore slower, than the paved road, but the thick woods might provide some shelter from the weather, and at least she wouldn't feel like a walking target. Out in plain sight on the road, she might as well have a bull's-eye painted on the back of her blue windbreaker.

The thick, tall trees did provide some protection from the torrents of rain spilling out of the sky, but she had no flashlight with her and couldn't see very well. Fortunately, there was a path, and although the mud and deepening puddles prevented her from hurrying, she did feel a little safer in the woods.

The heavy rain had softened the earth beneath her feet into a soggy goo. Walking was difficult. She slid as often as she stepped safely. Low-hanging branches she couldn't see in the darkness jumped out at her, snagging her hair, scratching her face. Several times she hit low spots in the path and sank up to her ankles in cold water and mud. The mud clung to her feet like glue, making her sodden shoes feel as if they were encased in cement. But she struggled on, because she had no choice.

The first couple of times she heard a noise behind her she told herself it was her imagination. The next time she heard it — a soft, padding sound — she told herself it was probably a small animal, a raccoon or a possum. But when the sound came again an uncomfortable feeling began to rise in her throat.

She was not alone in the woods. Someone was following her. The tire-slasher?

She stopped to listen intently. A fluttering sound in the trees overhead reminded her that bats had recently been reported in the area. The reports had frightened her, but Sam had dismissed her fears by saying, "It's not like you make a habit of wandering around outside after dark."

Well, no, not usually. Only when all four tires on her car had been slashed.

There! The sound came again, close enough to be heard distinctly. And it *was* footsteps, she was sure of it. It was an exact echo of the plodding, slogging, dragging-through-the-mud sound she herself was making.

Panicking, she tried to hurry. Her heart was

pounding so thunderously in her chest she was sure her pursuer could hear it. But she couldn't quiet her terror.

The sound behind her drew closer. Soft, soft . . .

Frantic, and sobbing quietly, she tried desperately to run. But her skirt, sweater, and jacket, completely saturated with water, weighed on her like a suit of solid lead. And her feet were imprisoned in a thick coat of gooey mud. Every step she took was a struggle, requiring enormous effort. Running was impossible.

"Te-ess! Oh, Te-ess!"

The voice, so close behind her, shocked her to a standstill. Distorted by the wind and the rain, the voice was unrecognizable. And evil. It was hard to believe that someone she knew well, a friend, could sound like that.

"Te-ess! Wait for me-ee!"

The sing-song was cruel, that of a predator who knows his prey is close at hand — and defenseless. *You'll have to be punished . . .*

Tess almost gave up. Soaked to the skin, with water dripping from her hair into her eyes, and mud up to her ankles, surrounded by dark, silent woods and sheets of rain, she thought about simply sinking to the soft ground and waiting for her tormentor to pounce on her. At least then she'd find out who it was.

No! Maybe he would catch up with her, maybe she didn't have a chance, maybe he was too cunning to be outsmarted. But she wasn't giving up without a fight!

Instead of continuing along the path, she veered abruptly, into the deeper, thicker woods sheltering a housing development. She would soon be trespassing on private property, but even a vicious guard dog would be better than what was behind her and closing in rapidly.

She emerged from the woods to see clumps of pale light ahead of her. A surge of hope overtook her. If she could just get to one of those houses . . .

Renewed hope quickened her steps. The lights grew larger, brighter. She heard a dog barking close by, and turned in that direction. A dog meant a dog owner and a dog owner meant a house and a house meant safety.

Safety. What a beautiful, wonderful word!

She was going to make it.

As she took a step forward, there was a sudden rustling sound behind her and something hit her between the shoulder blades. Already unsure of her footing, the blow threw her off balance, and she fell.

Expecting to hit the ground at any second, she braced herself for the sudden, unpleasant contact with a cold and muddy earth.

Instead, she felt a rush of air and the sensation of space all around her as the earth disappeared beneath her.

She had tumbled into open space. And she was falling, falling. . . .

Chapter 19

I could have finished her off tonight. Easily. But it's too soon. I have other plans to carry out before I take care of Tess.

No guilt. This is simple justice. What those men did was atrocious, and they can't be forgiven. They would never have been punished at all if I hadn't found the journal.

I read for so many hours that day in the lousy light of the attic, that my head felt like it was ready to split open. But I had to finish. By that time, it was as if she were writing only to me. And I had this feeling that she knew I was reading it.

The baby was born yesterday, right here in the trailer, with the help of Buddy's doctor. But I never even saw my baby! The doctor snatched the baby away the minute it was born, and gave me a shot. I was asleep in a minute or two and when I woke up, hours later, they were gone. All of them. Buddy, the doctor, and my baby. Gone!

Buddy showed up at the door later that night. When I asked him where my baby was, he said, "In its new home." Then he laid something on the dresser, saying it was a "gift" from the grateful parents, and left, warning me that if I made any attempt to see my baby or reveal who I was, I'd go to prison for a long, long time.

I just sat there in the dark after he left. Then I got up and walked to the dresser. I picked up the gift from the new parents.

It was a check. For a great deal of money. I had sold my baby. I hadn't meant to, but that was what I'd done.

I tore the check into a million pieces. They're here, those pieces, taped into the back of this book. They're the only proof I have of what happened. And I've taped in a list of the names of the others, besides Buddy, who were involved.

I can't fight them. The people who stole The Boardwalk and took my baby are too powerful. Going up against them would be a losing battle. I'm too tired for such a fight. My strength left me for good when they took my baby.

So I'm going to follow Tully. My child will be cared for, and I can only pray that the cruelty its new father showed me will not be exercised on my baby. Can such a man ever love? I can only pray that he can, he and his wife.

Perhaps, some day, someone will find these writings and understand my story. In that hope, I'm hiding this journal in my secret place.

And now, I go to Tully, with a prayer that he, and God, will forgive me.

That was the last entry.

I flipped the pages to the back cover. There, in a small plastic bag fastened with yellowed cellophane tape, were the pieces of paper Lila had talked about, shreds of the check Buddy had left on the dresser after he had taken her baby. And underneath the plastic bag was the list of names she'd mentioned. Every single one of them was familiar. Including my *own* last name. No surprise there. This was just the kind of thing I'd expect my father to be involved in.

Carefully setting the journal aside, I went downstairs to get my own roll of cellophane tape. I was very good at puzzles. I would put the pieces of the baby's "purchase price" together. And I would have the answer I needed.

Chapter 20

Tess's landing, when it came, was softened by a cushion of muddy water. But still it shocked her, knocking her breathless as she landed on her stomach, face down. Upon impact Tess was completely covered in thick, brown sludge. Pulling herself to a sitting position, she scrubbed her face frantically with her sleeve, and realized she was sitting in several inches of rainwater and mud.

Stunned and shaken, Tess slowly became aware of two other things. One, she was at the bottom of a huge, rectangular mudhole and two, there was a dog somewhere above her, barking furiously. The sound comforted her. With an angry dog close by, would the person who had pushed her dare return?

The first thing she needed to do, she decided, shaking her head to clear it, was escape from this watery prison. Dog or no dog, she couldn't stay down here.

But the walls of sodden earth were as slippery

as glass. Clawing at them desperately provided her-with nothing but two thick mittens of mud and deep frustration. Getting a foothold on the walls was equally impossible.

Still, she kept trying, slipping and sliding from spot to spot, searching with her hands and feet for something solid to grasp.

It was hopeless. Giving up, she moved away from the wall and shouted in fury through the sheets of rain to the barking dog, "Quit that stupid barking and go get some help! Didn't you ever hear of Lassie?" Then, her anger spent, she sank to her knees, tears of frustration and fear mixing with the rain on her face.

The barking stopped.

A fluttering in the air overhead stopped her heart. Bats! She screamed and covered her head with her hands, trying to shrink her body into as small and invisible a target as possible.

Suddenly, a beam of light shone down upon her and a deep voice called from above, "Hey, down there! Couldn't you wait until the pool was finished?"

Tess shrank back in fear. Who was that? Could it be the person who had been chasing her, who had sent her sailing into this watery hole?

"You okay? I'll get you out of there, hang on!"

No, this voice belonged to an older person. She didn't think it was anyone she knew. Maybe she could trust him. She almost laughed aloud hysterically. Wasn't that backwards? Weren't you supposed to be able to trust the people you knew, but not talk to strangers? How had everything gotten so screwed up?

"Please!" she called, "please get me out of here! Hurry!"

Something dangled in front of her. She reached out for it. It was a thick rope, waving like a flag of freedom before her.

"Can you climb that?" the voice called.

"No." She couldn't. Her strength was gone.

"You weigh much?" The voice belonged to a man. A big, strong one, she hoped.

"No. I'm skinny."

"Okay then. Just grab on, tight as you can, and I'll haul you up."

Tess obeyed. But her normally light weight had been increased by sodden clothing and several layers of mud. The haul upward went slowly. She tried to keep her body away from the wall, but there was nothing solid for her feet to push against, and her face slammed into the oozing wall more than once. Sputtering and spitting, she held onto the rope with every ounce of energy she had left. And finally, finally, she was on firm ground, her weary, shaken body supported by strong arms.

"How on earth did you land down there?" her rescuer asked, removing his tan raincoat and wrapping it around her. He was a big man, and he smiled at her as his flashlight revealed the mud monster she had become.

"I'm sorry," she said, her teeth chattering, "that I used your pool without your permission. I promise it will never happen again."

He laughed, and she recognized him. Trudy Slaughter's father. She had fallen into Trudy's pool?

"You're Mr. Slaughter, aren't you?" she asked as he half led, half carried her toward the house.

"Right. Do I know you? Not that anyone would recognize you right now."

"I'm Tess Landers."

"Guy Joe's girl? You go to school with Trudy, right? Well, Guy Joe's girl, how did you get into my pool?"

She couldn't say she'd been pushed. An answer like that would lead to too many questions, maybe even a visit from the police. She had no answers for them. Besides, she couldn't be that sure that someone had actually pushed her. It could have been a tree branch, blown by the wind, that hit her.

Sure. And The Boardwalk was the safest place in the world.

She couldn't help wondering, now that she knew how close Trudy lived to these woods, had *she* been the one stalking Tess?

Mr. Slaughter was waiting for an answer to his question.

"My car broke down," she said. "I was taking a shortcut home, but I didn't have a flashlight and I guess I got lost."

He nodded. "Hard to see on a night like this. Good thing Beau here doesn't like intruders."

The dog, a sleek Doberman pinscher, trotted along beside them, apparently satisfied that he'd performed his duty well.

When they reached the house, Mr. Slaughter wanted Tess to come inside. "Trudy isn't home, but I'm sure she'd want you to borrow some dry clothes."

Well, of course she wasn't home, Tess thought. She couldn't go running home so soon after pushing Tess into the pool. She'd have to wait a while, so that no one would know she'd ever been nearby. And Tess had no intention of setting one foot inside Trudy Slaughter's house.

"I'd really rather go home, Mr. Slaughter. If you could find an old blanket or something to cover the seat, maybe you could drive me home? I wouldn't want to ruin your upholstery, abominable mudman that I am right now."

He didn't argue with her. Tess suspected that he might have if he'd known that Shelley was out of town and Tess was going home to an empty house. So she didn't volunteer that piece of information.

When they pulled up in front of the condo, Sam's car was parked beside the stone patio wall. And Sam was in it.

He got out when the Slaughter car arrived. Tess was grateful that he didn't laugh as she got out of the car. He didn't look much better, though. He was almost as wet and mud-covered as she was. Her heart sank. Could he have been running around in the woods? After *her*, maybe?

All of this suspicion was making her crazy.

"That your brother?" Mr. Slaughter asked as she got out of the car.

"No. That's Sam Oliver."

"Oh. Trent's boy. Friend of yours, I guess. You'll be okay, then?"

Friend? Who could be sure? "It's okay, Mr. Slaughter," she said, reaching into the car to hand him his raincoat. "I'll be fine now. Thanks for everything. And thank Beau for me. Maybe I'll buy him a nice big bone."

Apparently convinced that Tess was in good hands with "Trent's boy," Mr. Slaughter drove away.

"What happened to you?" Sam asked, removing his windbreaker and draping it across her shoulders. "You look like you just had a mud bath."

"Close," she said cryptically. Then she moved to sweep past him with as much dignity as she could muster, but he stepped directly in front of her, blocking her path.

The words *Who will be next?* swam in front of her eyes again, and she felt dizzy. Not Sam, she prayed, don't let it be Sam.

"I'll take you to your father's," he said. "You can get cleaned up there and get a good night's sleep."

No. Maybe she would go to her father's. Soon. She did want to ask him if any employees had been fired recently from The Boardwalk. But she wasn't getting in a car with anyone. Not until she knew who was sending her purple poetry and making nasty phone calls and following her.

Because it might not have been Trudy. It could have been Sam.

"I can get cleaned up right here in my own

house," she said defiantly. "We have plenty of soap and water."

"You're going to stay here alone tonight? I went to the hospital to see if you'd left yet, and I saw what someone did to your car, Tess. That was deliberate. Did you call the police?"

"No. Not yet." And she wasn't going to, either. But she didn't have to tell him that.

"Tess, how did you get so muddy? Something happened, didn't it? I knew it! Beak said you'd be okay, but Candace was pretty worried when I told her about your tires."

"Was Trudy with them?" If Trudy had been with Candace and Beak, she couldn't have been running around in the woods pushing people into unfinished swimming pools.

"Uh-uh. Beak and Candace were at Amy's, scarfing down ice cream." He frowned. "Weren't you just with Trudy? That *was* Kevin Slaughter who brought you home, wasn't it? Trudy's old man?"

They were getting even wetter, with only the driveway lampposts for protection from the weather. "I'm going inside," she said, moving around him toward the patio gate. "Go home." So Trudy hadn't been at Amy's with Beak and Candace. Maybe she'd been too busy for ice cream. *Busy hunting.*

"Tess . . ."

She stopped and turned around.

"I talked to my dad tonight. He said Chalmers will be releasing a statement tomorrow that The Devil's Elbow crash was an 'unavoidable accident.' "

Tess snorted rudely.

"Maybe it was, Tess."

"Since when do you take your father's or Chalmers's word for anything?" she asked rudely. "You never listen to your father, and you were the one who said Chalmers couldn't find his own nose without a mirror. You're also the one who said they'd cover up whatever they found and now when they're doing just that, you're taking their side."

"There isn't any side, Tess. This isn't a war."

She looked straight at him, her chin thrust forward defiantly, tears sliding from the corners of her eyes. "Oh, isn't it?" Then she turned and hurried into the house, slamming the door after her.

She didn't watch to see if he left. Instead, she went through her door-and-window-locking ritual, called a garage to have her car picked up, and headed for the bathroom for a long, hot, comforting shower.

The shower renewed her spirits slightly, and she was about to make a cup of hot tea, when the telephone rang. Setting the blue-and-white teakettle on the kitchen counter, she picked up the phone. If it was Shelley, maybe she'd just give her a piece of her mind, tell her exactly what she thought of parents who left their children to traipse halfway around the world when there were crazy people running loose!

"Happy birthday to Trudy," sang that voice that sent shivers down Tess's spine. "Happy birthday to Trudy, happy birthday to Trudy, may she live till you die!" Then the voice added in a low sing-song,

"Which may be soo-on!" Then the line went dead.

Tess held the silent telephone in her hand a moment or two longer. Then she slowly replaced it in its berth on the wall. Turning, she picked up the teakettle, placed it on a stove burner and switched on the heat. Staring at the gas flames as if hypnotized, she repeated in her head the words she'd just heard on the phone.

Something terrible was going to happen at Trudy's party.

Chapter 21

Liars! They're going to announce that The Devil's Elbow crash was accidental. They know it wasn't. There was no loose rail. It was my lead pipe that sent that roller coaster into space.

What good does it do me to punish them if they let the whole town think nothing is going on?

Well, not the whole town. Tess knows. She doesn't know why, but she knows nothing was accidental. She just doesn't know what to do about it.

It's time to do something that can't be interpreted, even by Chalmers and the board, as accidental. Shake them up a little.

They're worried, I know they are. They had a meeting here last night. The driveway looked like a luxury-car dealership. I thought about eavesdropping and decided against it. What could I overhear that I didn't already know? And after the meeting, I ran into my father in the upstairs hall and saw his eyes go to the attic door. Is he beginning to remember about the journal? Why didn't he get rid of it a long time ago? Ego, maybe. Didn't want to let go of the only real proof of his greatest accomplishment.

If he does remember, and looks for the journal, he won't find it. I've hidden it. When my plan is finished, I'll send it to someone I trust, so that none of the men involved can find it and destroy it. The people of Santa Luisa have a right to the truth. Just as I had a right to it. But it was kept from me.

Until Lila told me. Through her written words.

It didn't take me very long to Scotch tape that shredded check together. When the puzzle was completed, there was the signature, big as life.

I'd seen that signature many times before. It had signed my report cards and permission slips for school outings and a number of checks exactly like the one I held Scotch taped in front of me, given to me in place of birthday presents. It was a name I knew well. *Very* well.

It was my father's name.

The attic began to spin around me. My father had "bought" a baby. Considering Lila O'Hare's account, *stolen* was a better word. He'd stolen a baby.

And then I looked at the date on the check. It was my birthday.

Suddenly everything was clear. I wasn't who I thought I was.

My last name wasn't the same as the signature on the check, after all. Not really. My last name was O'Hare.

I was the O'Hare baby.

Chapter 22

On Friday, Tess's car was delivered, complete with four brand-new tires. And a brief announcement on the radio and in the newspaper that the crash of The Devil's Elbow had been due to a "loose rail," which would be quickly repaired, ended speculation in Santa Luisa about recent events at The Boardwalk.

When Tess questioned Gina at the hospital about how her own accident was being explained, Gina shrugged and said, "I guess I fell over the railing." And when Tess looked plainly disgusted by that answer, Gina continued, "Tess, I wish you'd quit worrying about it. It's over and done with, and I'm going home soon. You'll drive yourself nuts if you don't forget about it. Daddy said The Devil's Elbow will be good as new and we won't even remember the crash happened after a while. I'll be good as new, too. Can't you relax?"

Tess couldn't. Completely convinced that both accidents had been anything but accidental, but not having a shred of proof, she felt helpless and frightened. This wasn't the end of it, she was sure of that. There was more to come.

She went to Trudy's birthday party on Saturday, hoping to learn something. The people attending all had parents on the board. If she kept her eyes and ears open, maybe she'd come up with some answers. But she went with a sense of dread that something bad was going to happen. She was convinced the phone call hadn't been a joke.

The party was held at night, on the beach below The Boardwalk. Darkness had fallen before Trudy's guests arrived, but the area was bathed in the amusement park's neon glow, with additional lighting provided by tall pole lamps scattered along the beach. The rain had temporarily ceased, and only a few innocent-looking clouds floated now and again across the half moon. A Saturday night with nothing to do in Santa Luisa, combined with the results of Chalmers's investigation, had brought increased business to The Boardwalk. Laughter and music, along with the usual smells of hot dogs, popcorn, and cotton candy, gave the party site the proper atmosphere.

When Tess arrived, Sam and Guy Joe, in cutoffs and short-sleeved sweatshirts, had already built a small, cozy fire. Trudy, unsuitably dressed for a picnic in an elegant yellow jumpsuit, her hair piled on top of her head, sat in a lawn chair like, Tess thought to herself, a queen waiting to greet her subjects. And Candace, cocooned in a dull blue muumuu, busied herself removing food items from a wicker hamper. Several blankets were spread close together to provide seating and some slight protection against the rain-dampened sand.

Doss arrived shortly after Tess. Beak came next, a huge bouquet of multicolored balloons in hand. Presenting them to Trudy with a dramatic flourish, he asked where the food was.

"Here, Beak," Trudy said, offering him a red box crammed full of chocolate-frosted brownies. "Take this temptation out of my path. We're not having hot dogs until I open my presents, but you can start with these. If I eat even one, the chocolate will go straight to my hips."

Beak selected two very large brownies. Then he donned a party hat of pink crepe paper trimmed with silver and began dancing on the sand, his mouth full of brownie, arms and legs flailing to music from the cassette player Trudy had brought. Grabbing another tiny hat, this one bright yellow, he slid its thin elastic band over his head and clamped the pointed little hat over his nose.

Laughing at his antics, Tess found it hard to imagine that this silly, crazy boy could have had anything to do with sabotaging The Boardwalk.

Then Trudy cried, "Beak, you look like a psychotic chicken!" which wiped the smile from Tess's face. *Psychotic* wasn't a word to be thrown around too lightly these days. And Beak hadn't laughed when Trudy said it. Hadn't he heard her? Or had he decided to ignore it because it hit too close to home?

A sudden hand on her shoulder startled her and she jumped and whirled around.

"For Pete's sake!" Sam said. "Relax! You're as nervous as my old man when the stock market takes a dive. What's the matter with you?"

"Nothing." She twisted a strand of hair around her finger nervously. "But you shouldn't sneak up on people like that."

"Sneak up? You looked lonesome standing over here all by yourself. How come you haven't joined the party?"

Because I don't trust anyone, she wanted to answer, but didn't. Because I'm waiting for doom to strike, her mouth got ready to say, but didn't. Because . . .

"I thought you'd be more relaxed now," Sam said, watching her face carefully, "now that we know The Devil's Elbow crash was accidental."

She laughed harshly. "Yeah, that's a big relief, isn't it?"

"You still don't believe it?"

Beak ran over to Candace and tugged at her hand, insisting that she join him in his crazy dance. To Tess's surprise, Candace did.

"Sure, I believe it," Tess lied, because she couldn't tolerate one more person telling her to forget about it. "Any reason why I shouldn't?"

He knew she was lying, and looked hurt. "No, I guess not. Take a walk down to the water with me."

"No." She wasn't going near the water. A drowning would make a great "accident," wouldn't it? Besides, she should stay here. Since she was the only one who expected something bad to happen, she needed to keep her eyes open. Maybe if she really paid attention, she could somehow prevent another disaster.

"Well, then walk up the beach a little way with me. C'mon."

She hesitated, watching Doss. He seemed uncomfortable, sitting off to one side of the blankets by himself. She knew he had come only to please Gina. Just as Trudy had probably invited him only to please Gina. Although, who knew about Trudy? Maybe she had a reason for wanting all of them there. Doss's father was no longer on the board of directors, but he *had* been. Maybe that was why Doss had been included at Trudy's party.

On the other hand, if it was Doss who had caused the crash and taken the saucer and made the telephone calls and sent the ugly note, this would be the perfect opportunity for him to do more damage. With Gina safely in the hospital, he wouldn't have to worry about accidentally hurting her while he was targeting any of the others.

She wished with all her heart that this evening was already over, and they were all safely back in their own homes.

"Trudy hasn't opened her presents yet," she told Sam.

"Yeah, I noticed. She's too wrapped up in your brother to unwrap presents. Hey, a little play on words there? Wrapped up, unwrap, get it?"

"I got it. I just didn't think it was very funny."

"It wasn't supposed to be funny. It was an accident."

That word again. *Accident.* She had learned to hate it.

Laughter from The Boardwalk echoed out over the beach. People were having fun up there. She wished she could join them. "I wish Trudy would open her presents and feed us. I'm starved!" She was stalling. The thought of food sickened her.

"Have a brownie."

"Too sweet. I want real food." Something as sweet and gooey as a brownie would be worse than trying to swallow ordinary food. "She promised us hot dogs."

"Well, while we're waiting, take a walk with me."

Beak and Candace were still cavorting on the sand, Guy Joe was being held captive by Trudy, and Doss was delving into the brownie box. He seemed to have relaxed a little and he didn't look the least bit dangerous.

Maybe she could leave them alone for a few minutes. It would give her a chance to explain her theory about the board of directors to Sam. If he laughed at her, she'd simply never speak to him again. But if he didn't, maybe together they could figure out what to do. They wouldn't walk very far.

"Okay. But just for a few minutes." Casting one last quick glance across the party group to make sure everything was okay, Tess turned and joined Sam. "And we can't go far."

They plodded silently across the damp sand. The night wind tugged gently at her hair, sent her short, full red skirt billowing around her legs. Because she had her head down, Tess didn't notice until too late that they had been walking toward the disabled Devil's Elbow. The lights trimming its lengthy frame were still on, but the tracks were bare, the cardboard signs still waving on the thick rope fence.

"I don't want to be here," Tess said clearly, stopping in her tracks. "Let's go back."

"Don't be silly, Tess." Sam looked down at her, annoyance bringing his brows together. "The thing isn't even working now. The new cars haven't been delivered yet. What's there to be scared of?"

"It gives me the creeps, that's all. Makes me jittery just looking at it." And it did. She kept hearing the screams . . .

"You're turning into a nervous wreck," he accused gently. "Everybody says so. If you don't relax — "

"Of course I'm a nervous wreck!" she shouted, losing control. "And you would be, too, if you had half a brain! Haven't you even noticed that the kids hurt the worst so far all have parents on The Boardwalk's board of directors?"

He hadn't. She could tell by the startled look on his face. "What?"

"And that's something they all have in common with *you*," she continued. "Your father is a director, too. So is mine." Her voice rose again, "So why *aren't* you a nervous wreck?"

Sam began walking in a small circle around her, his head down. "Never even crossed my mind," he said. "What made you come up with such a crazy theory?"

"Facts, Sam, facts," she said crossly. "Can't you *see* it? Can't you even admit that it's a possibility? That someone is out to ruin The Boardwalk and hurt a lot of people at the same time? It's the only answer that makes sense."

He stopped pacing to look at her. "Got any idea who it might be? This crazy phantom of yours? And why he's freaked out?"

She shook her head. "I have a couple of possibilities, but no proof. And it's no phantom, Sam. Phantoms don't send threatening notes and make nasty phone calls." She should have kept the note. It was more convincing than anything she could say. Too late now.

"Look," he said, "I'm not saying you're right or you're wrong. But if you're even close to the truth, why haven't you moved back to your father's house? You'd be safe there. I don't see how you can think what you think and still stay alone in that condo out there in the woods. Makes no sense."

She had been thinking about doing exactly that, moving back with her father and Guy Joe, just until this nightmare was over. But if Sam wasn't convinced that her theory was a valid one, what business did he have accusing her of being foolish? Either there was a reason to be afraid or there wasn't. Sam couldn't have it both ways.

"Then you agree that my theory makes sense?"

"I didn't say that. But if *you* think it does, why are you still in the condo? If Chalmers and the board are covering up something, this is no time for someone like you to be all alone out there in the woods."

"Someone like me? What's that supposed to mean?" Occasionally biting her nails and twisting her hair didn't mean she needed a keeper! He was being so patronizing, she thought angrily.

"Someone," he said firmly, "who gets spooked just looking at a roller coaster that isn't even working. Why are you being so stubborn about this?"

"And why can't you take me seriously?" she shouted. "Why can't you admit that everything I've said makes sense?"

In exasperation, he reached out and took hold of her shoulders, as if he was about to shake her. Instead, he pulled her close to him, bent his head, and kissed her. "There," he said as she pushed him away, "is that taking you seriously enough?"

The kiss had unsettled her. Flustered, she said angrily, "What is that, some kind of therapy for people you consider nervous wrecks? Well, it didn't work. I still think I'm right, and until you do, too, I don't want to talk to you. Go away!"

"Oh, I give up!" he shouted in disgust, and turned in the sand to stride away from her, throwing his hands up in the air as he walked.

She watched until he became a blurred shadow in the darkness. She was sorry she'd ever agreed to take a walk with him.

Why hadn't he been willing to discuss her question about the victims being kids of the board of directors? It was worth discussing. It could be the key to this whole, ugly business.

She was *not* going to follow him. Not yet. No trailing after him like a lost puppy. She wasn't wild about staying out here under The Devil's Elbow by herself, but it was better than following Sam as if he were her keeper. She'd sit on the sand for a while to cool off, and then rejoin the party. Laughter and music rang out from the place where Trudy was celebrating her birthday. It sounded like fun. She'd go back in a few minutes.

The sand was damp, and soothed her fingers as she dug into it, molding little hills on either side of her as she watched the surf teasing the shore.

Her left hand touched something hard and sharp, buried in the sand. She pulled out the object and turned toward The Boardwalk to give herself more light. The object appeared to be a small stone — some type of gem. Holding it up to the light, Tess saw that it was blue. And she'd seen stones like this before. It wasn't particularly valuable, she was sure of that. It was something very common.

Of course! It was the kind of stone worn in Santa Luisa High School class rings. She'd bought hers early in September. But it had proved to be so bulky that she seldom wore it, keeping it instead in her jewelry box.

Someone in town wasn't wearing theirs at all. A class ring would look pretty stupid with the stone missing.

She stood up, stone in hand. She looked around, frowning. And looked down at the spot where she'd been sitting. It was directly beneath that last gentle curve in The Devil's Elbow's tracks.

That probably meant nothing, Tess tried to assure herself. Everyone in town wore Santa Luisa

High class rings. And stones probably fell out of them all the time.

Or did it mean the stone belonged to the person who had tampered with the roller coaster?

Anyway, the stone couldn't be identified. Only the rings were identifiable. And she didn't have the ring belonging to this stone.

But she slipped the stone into the pocket of her red long-sleeved shirt. She couldn't have said why. It seemed the right thing to do.

Then she hurried back to the party.

She was halfway there when the quiet hit her. There was supposed to be a party going on ahead of her, but there was no noise. Quiet as a tomb. That didn't make sense. Where had the laughter, the music gone?

Her steps quickened. They hadn't left without her, had they? Left her alone out here? No, they wouldn't do that. Guy Joe wouldn't.

Then, half running across the hard-packed sand, she heard sounds coming from the direction of the blankets.

But they weren't party sounds.

The sounds she heard were moans and groans, sounds of pain. Almost like a muted version of the sounds she'd heard on the boardwalk the night The Devil's Elbow had crashed.

Heart pounding, she ran the last few steps.

And arrived on the scene to find everyone but Sam and Trudy writhing in agony on the sand, clutching their stomachs and moaning in pain.

Chapter 23

Tess ran to Sam and clutched at his elbow. "What? What's happening? What's wrong with them?" she cried, her eyes on her agonized friends.

"Don't know. They just doubled over all of a sudden, a second ago. Trudy," he barked, "get an ambulance! Hurry!"

Trudy ran. When she had gone, Tess turned to Sam in tears. "I didn't want to be right about something bad happening. I *didn't!*"

"I know that," he said, putting an arm around her shoulders. "Let's see if we can do something for them."

But the only thing they could do was cover everyone with a jacket or sweater, and wait.

When Trudy returned, breathless, she began wringing her hands as she saw that nothing had changed. "I can't believe this is happening!" she shrieked. "What is the *matter* with them?" Then her eyes narrowed in suspicion, focusing on Beak, who was rolling from side to side on the sand, moaning. "Beak, if this is one of your practical jokes, I swear I'll strangle you! You're ruining my party."

"Get real, Trudy!" Sam snapped as sirens began, once again, to approach The Boardwalk. "Look at their faces. Does it look like anyone's joking?"

Tess, thinking wearily that she would be hearing sirens in her sleep for the rest of her life, knelt by Guy Joe's side. His pain was so great he had bitten through his bottom lip. A thin stream of blood pooled on his chin. She took one of his hands in hers, but he gripped it so hard, she cried out in pain and he let go. Tess hadn't felt so helpless since the night she'd been trapped in the muddy, unfinished swimming pool.

Sam bent over her. "Did you eat any brownies?" he asked, his voice low.

"What?" What was taking that ambulance so long?

"I said, did you eat any of those brownies Trudy passed around?"

"No. I wanted real food, remember? Why?"

Sam crouched beside her. A distraught Trudy was tossing party things into bags and baskets, muttering in distress to herself, and the injured were too preoccupied with their pain to listen to Sam. Still, he kept his voice low. "Because I didn't eat any, either. And I'm fine. And Trudy's on a diet. But Beak and Guy Joe each polished off a couple of pieces, and Doss had at least one. So did Candace. Get the picture?"

Before she could concentrate on the meaning of Sam's words, the ambulance arrived.

When the attendants had asked about booze and drugs and been assured that none of either were used at the party, Sam handed one of the paramedics the red box, now empty of all but a small chunk of chocolatey cookie. "Brownies," he said brusquely. "They ate them. We didn't."

Asking no further questions, the attendants took the red box with them when they drove away with the patients.

Sam, Trudy, and Tess followed the ambulance in Sam's car. They were sitting in the now familiar waiting room when the parents of the victims began rushing in.

"Tess," her father demanded when he arrived, "what is going on? What's happened to your brother? And where were you when it happened?" He was, as always, impeccably dressed in tan slacks and a pale blue sweater. His thick white hair was perfectly in place. And his blue eyes were as cold as ice.

"I was there," she answered defensively. "And to answer your next question, it wasn't drugs or booze. It was probably brownies."

Thick, white eyebrows aimed for the sky. "Brownies?"

"Trudy had a box of them at the party. Everyone who ate them got sick," Tess elaborated, sinking back into her orange plastic chair.

"Are you talking about ptomaine poisoning?" he demanded. "Who made these brownies?"

"I guess they were a gift," she said vaguely.

"Only we don't know who from. From whom. There wasn't any card on the box. Trudy said she found it sitting on the picnic hamper."

The other parents had joined Tess and her father and were listening intently to every word. Mrs. Beecham, wearing a very expensive-looking but outdated black dress and black shoes with worn heels, hovered on the edge of the group as if unsure of her welcome. Beak's parents, whose formal clothing told Tess they'd probably been enjoying a Saturday night at the Country Club, looked concerned, and Sam's father, in golf clothes, stood beside his son, looking annoyed.

"Are you *sure* you weren't fooling around with drugs?" Mrs. Rapp asked Trudy. "We have, of course, always considered the possibility that Robert might experiment with controlled substances. And he hasn't been himself lately. He seems angry about something, and has been remarkably rude lately. His younger sisters have just about had it with him."

"No drugs!" a teary-eyed Trudy shouted. "We said it wasn't drugs or booze and it wasn't."

"No, it wasn't," a strange voice agreed. The voice came from the doorway.

All heads turned. A tall, thin man in a white jacket came toward them. He wore glasses and carried a clipboard.

"Doctor Joe Tanner," he said. "I've been pumping the kids' stomachs. They'll be okay. Miserable, but okay. We'll keep them here overnight to make sure there's no permanent damage." Then looking at Mrs. Rapp, he added, "These kids are telling you the truth. It wasn't drugs or booze. Their friends were poisoned."

There was a stunned silence. Sam looked over at Tess, the expression on his face grim.

"Poisoned?" Trudy asked in a small voice. "You mean it wasn't just someone making a mistake when they baked the brownies? Like putting in too much of something or not enough of something else?"

The doctor shook his head. "This was no accident, if that's what you mean. Looks like rat poison, although we can't be sure until the lab has analyzed the remaining brownie. But it's definitely poison. Fast-acting." He looked down at the chart in his hands. "Is there a Beecham here?"

Mrs. Beecham moved forward hesitantly.

"Your son can go home tonight. Donald, that's his name?"

She nodded. "Doss. Everyone calls him Doss."

"He must not have consumed as much of the tainted food as the others. Very minor damage to his gastrointestinal system. I'm releasing him."

Maybe the reason Doss wasn't very hungry, Tess thought angrily, was that he *knew* the brownies weren't exactly a health food. And if someone had poisoned food at a party and wanted to avoid suspicion, wouldn't that someone eat just a little bit of that food? Enough to make that someone look like one of the victims?

Was that what Doss had done?

"Are you telling us," Tess's father asked, "that someone tried to *kill* my son?"

Tess shot him a look of disgust. Wasn't it just like him to see the problem only in terms of himself? There were two other boys and a girl in that emergency room.

"No." Dr. Tanner shook his head. "I'm not telling you that. There wasn't enough poison in any of the kids to kill them. Either the guilty party didn't know his toxicology, or he never intended to take anyone's life. Just make them suffer. A lot."

Tess tried to take it all in. Poison! No way could this be called an accident. It had been deliberate. The doctor had said so.

"I've got to get back," the doctor said. "But the police are here and I think they want to talk to all of you, so don't leave, okay?"

Sam and Trudy and Tess nodded silently.

When he had gone, taking the parents with him, a depressed silence fell over the group. Trudy was crying quietly in a corner. But Tess wasn't impressed. Trudy Slaughter had acted the lead in several plays at school. And she'd been very good. Very convincing.

Those brownies had shown up at *her* party. She'd told Tess tearfully that they'd been a gift. But there hadn't been a card.

Trudy could very well have brought them herself.

"Poison," Tess said, in almost a whisper. "I can't believe it." She stared at the white tiled floor and twisted her hair around a finger.

"*Now* will you move back with your dad?" Sam

asked. "This waiting room has been a second home to us lately. I've been thinking of installing my toothbrush in the bathroom down the hall. But if I have to come here again, I don't want it to be because of you."

She lifted her head. "I'll think about it, I promise. But I'm not going back tonight, because Guy Joe won't be there. I don't want to be alone in that house with my father. Maybe I'll go up and see Gina. She should be told about this before she hears gossip around the hospital. And maybe I'll spend the night in a chair in her room. That way, I'd be close to Guy Joe, too." She didn't add, *And I'd be safe there*, although the thought certainly crossed her mind.

Just then Chief Chalmers, a heavyset, red-faced man who walked with a slight rolling motion, entered the room, followed by two other policemen.

Tess was glad to see them. The uniforms were reassuring, in spite of the fact that so far they hadn't been of much help to her. But they couldn't dismiss a deliberate poisoning the way they had the other incidents.

"You still got that cookie box?" the Chief asked when they'd filled him in on the evening's events.

Trudy shook her head. "We gave it to the ambulance attendants. You can get it from the doctor, I think."

Chief Chalmers, looking grim, told them he would want to talk to them again, after the toxicology report was in. Then he left, taking his companions with him.

"Well," Sam said when they'd gone, "at least he's not blowing off this one as a prank. That's something."

"I'm going up to see Gina, tell her what happened," Tess said. "You'd better take Trudy back to the beach to get her stuff." She wasn't worried about Sam being alone with Trudy, even if Trudy *had* poisoned the brownies. Sam could take care of himself.

Making her promise to call him before she left for her father's house with Guy Joe the next day, Sam left. Watching a thoroughly shaken Trudy follow him out of the waiting room, Tess found it hard to believe the girl was guilty. She seemed so upset by the disastrous end to her birthday party.

But then, she *was* an actress.

Tess had to sneak into Gina's room. She hadn't realized how late it was. Visiting hours were long over, the halls dim. Gina was sound asleep, with only a tiny nightlight on over her bed. Exhausted, but feeling perfectly safe for the first time in a long while, Tess curled up in a chair and fell asleep.

Chapter 24

The truth of who I was had danced around the attic that afternoon. I could feel it laughing at me. And as it came closer and closer, stealing my breath and wrapping itself around me, I felt every shred of the old me sliding out of my body and slipping along the attic's wooden floor until it disappeared through the cracks.

I was gone. There wasn't any *me* anymore. My whole life had been a lie and when the truth erased that lie, it erased me as well. I didn't exist.

How could I argue with the words of the woman who had lived this story, whose words spoke of truth and pain? How could I argue with the signed check with my father's signature on it? How could I protest a date that said, quite clearly, that although I had indeed been born when I thought I'd been, I hadn't been born *who* I thought I'd been?

I was the O'Hare baby. I was the baby snatched out of its mother's arms on the day it was born. I was the child lied to, never told the truth, never told who its real parents were. I was the kid who had every material possession possible but never an ounce of real love.

Lila O'Hare would have given me that love. I could tell that from her writing. And Tully would have, too, if my father and his friends hadn't driven the man to suicide.

I *wanted* that life, with Lila and Tully. I knew, I *knew* it would have been a good life.

But I couldn't have it now, not ever. It had been stolen from me, just as everything had been stolen from my real parents. They'd even stolen Lila's journal after she killed herself, and my "father" had hidden it here, his incredible ego unwilling or unable to part with it. I shivered, thinking of the horror of it.

The man I'd thought was my father, and his friends, had lied and lied. Because of that, my whole life was a lie. So what did it matter what I did with that lie of a life? No wonder I had never felt that I belonged with this man, belonged with this family. I *didn't*.

They had to be punished. All of them. But what could I do to them that would equal what they'd done to Lila, to Tully, and to me? What would be awful enough?

Suddenly, I knew the answer. It was almost as if a voice were whispering in my ear. "Don't punish the men," the voice said. "Punish their children. The men will suffer the most if you do this." I knew the voice was right.

And the children would be easy to get to. They were, without exception, my friends. I saw them all the time. They trusted me. Why shouldn't they? They didn't know what I knew.

That was how it all started. It's worked out pretty well, so far. And now, I've finally done something that can't be passed off as an accident. It'll be great fun watching Chalmers flounder around trying to explain it. No one will believe that what I did this time was an accident. No way.

It's kind of weird, knowing you're not real. Makes everything easy, in a way. Feels like I'm walking around without a body, as if I'm already in spirit form.

I will be, soon. I've decided that when I've finished with my list of targets, I'll join my real parents. Why not? I have no life here. Those people stole it from me. My life isn't my life anymore. So what's there to hold on to?

But before I go, Tess has to suffer. I've been keeping her scared so she'd seem crazy and no one would take her seriously. And it's worked. But she's not getting off that easily. I have to teach her a lesson.

Because Tess messed things up for me. Now I have to skip one of the names on my list. Chalmers will have to investigate this time and he could trace the poison to my house. The hardware store keeps a record of all poison sales. Chalmers could come knocking on my door any minute now.

What really makes me angry is that I never found out who Buddy was. That was so important. I'd ask around, but I can't afford to make people suspicious. And I certainly can't ask the one person who would definitely know. The man who used to be my father. No, I can't ask him.

But I got most of them. Sometimes I even got to see the pain in the parents' faces. That made it all worthwhile. I was happy to see them suffer! Serves them right. They can't suffer enough pain to satisfy me, after what they did. I wish I could have done more.

The only thing left to do is to punish Tess.

I'm going to take her with me when I go.

Chapter 25

Tess was gently shaken awake the following morning by Mrs. Giambone. "What on earth are you doing here?" she asked with concern, as Tess tried to remember the answer to that question. Before she succeeded, Gina awoke, and when she realized who was in the room, repeated her mother's question to Tess.

Struggling awake, rubbing her eyes fiercely and realizing that every muscle in her body ached, Tess explained.

Gina was horrified. "You'd better go and stay at my house until Chalmers comes up with some answers. Right, Mom?" she said, looking at her parent for confirmation.

But Tess said quickly, "No, it's okay. I'm going home with Guy Joe. I'll stay there until Shelley comes back." She reached up to smooth her hair into some sort of order. "You know that place. It's a fortress!" She was hoping Gina wouldn't ask who Tess thought was behind the poisoning, because she would have had to say Doss and/or Trudy, and she couldn't deal with Gina's reaction to her suspicions of Doss.

Telling Gina and her mother she'd be right back, Tess left the room to find out when Guy Joe was being discharged and how he intended to get home.

Guy Joe was in the shower, but his father was picking him up at nine-thirty, the nurse at the desk told her. Tess left him a note saying she'd be leaving with them and would come to his room before nine-thirty, and then she returned to Gina's room. She stayed long enough to fill Gina in on Trudy's party. There was no point in keeping the details from her, because the hospital would be buzzing with that information. Tess preferred that her best friend hear the gory details from her.

"I thought you were imagining things before," Gina said when Tess had finished. "But I guess you weren't. Something terrible is going on. And you suspect someone, don't you? I can tell. Who is it? *Tell* me!"

But Tess couldn't. What was the point in upsetting Gina? Tess had no proof. And Gina had enough problems right now. Pointing at the clock, she told Gina she had to get downstairs to meet her father and, promising to return later, left the room.

The ride home was a solemn one. The rain had eased, although the sky was gray enough to promise more later. Tess sat uncomfortably on the front seat between Guy Joe and her father. She was anxious to shower and change into clean, fresh clothes. After Guy Joe told her he was glad she hadn't eaten

142

any brownies and that he was feeling weak but fine, and she said she was sorry she couldn't have helped him more, the conversation died. The remainder of the ride was silent.

The only comment from their father was, "Chalmers had better do his job right this time, or I'll know the reason why."

Tess and Guy Joe simply nodded.

The big, red brick house looked gloomy and forbidding, but she told herself that was probably because of the weather. Still, it was hard to regard her father's home as a safe haven. Was any place safe right now?

At least she wouldn't be alone. And neither Doss nor Trudy could get at her here. They would never make it past the front gate.

When their father had deposited them at the front door, he went off to work. She and Guy Joe went straight to their rooms. Tess showered and crawled into bed, and was asleep in minutes. When the housekeeper, Maria, knocked on the door to awaken her for dinner, Tess was shocked to discover that the clock on her bedside table read six-thirty! She'd slept all day! Well, why not? The thought of leaving her fortress to go see Gina made her hands sweat and her heart pound. But she had promised.

Maybe she could talk Guy Joe into going to the hospital with her. If he felt up to it. If not, she'd call . . . who? Who did she trust enough to call? Candace, maybe. Although Candace probably wasn't feeling very well, either. I just can't go out alone, she thought, close to tears. I can't! It's too risky.

Dressing quickly in an old pair of jeans and the red top from the night before, she hurried downstairs.

Dinner was as quiet and unpleasant as the ride home had been. Telling herself it was worth it just to feel safe, Tess ate quickly and asked to be excused.

"I have a meeting tonight," her father said, not looking up from his chocolate mousse. "Robert Rapp is picking me up. You may use my car if you have somewhere to go."

That was a surprise. If Guy Joe wouldn't go with her, she could drive her father's Mercedes and someone watching for her little blue car would be disappointed. "I promised Gina I'd take her something to read. But I'll be back early." Then she remembered what she had wanted to ask him. "Father, I was wondering . . . have you or anyone else on the board fired someone recently?"

His white head lifted, blue eyes met hers. "No. No one besides Beecham. Why would you ask that?"

Tess felt her cheeks reddening. "Well, all of the kids hurt have parents on the board. Doesn't that seem awfully coincidental to you?"

"Exactly right," he said firmly, returning to his mousse. "Coincidence, nothing more. Chalmers will handle things. You go on and have a good time, now."

And that was that. He might as well have said,

"Run along and play now," she thought angrily. End of discussion.

Her father turned to Guy Joe. "Any plans tonight?"

"Nope. Not me," Guy Joe said, standing up. "I'm wiped out. I'm just going to sack out, take life easy."

Tess's heart sank. But she wouldn't push. She didn't blame him. He'd been through an awful experience last night.

Maybe she'd be safe in her father's car. Whoever was watching for her would think that Guy Joe, Sr., was in the Mercedes.

"Very well," her father said. "I'll see you both later." They'd been excused.

"He hasn't changed, has he?" Tess said quietly as she followed her brother up the stairs.

"Did you think he might have?" Guy Joe asked with a grin.

Tess shrugged. "Isn't hope supposed to spring eternal?"

"Not in this house."

Sighing heavily, she went on to her bedroom, planning to look for her old yearbooks. Gina would get a kick out of them.

They weren't there. Maria must have moved them. Put them somewhere out of the way, thinking Tess wasn't coming back.

Well, if she was going to have to search the house, she'd take her Walkman with her. That way, George Michael could keep her company and she wouldn't be disturbing Guy Joe's much-needed sleep. Clamping the headphones over her ears and snapping the cassette player on the metal chain belt circling the waist of her jeans, she began her search.

It took a while. The last room she entered was large and dark. New raindrops slid down the small windows. She switched on the overhead light, a bare bulb with a chain pull. But she had no idea where to begin looking. The yearbooks could be in any one of a dozen boxes and trunks. There, that trunk in the corner, maybe?

Before she could open it, she'd have to unload all that junk on the lid. What were all those things, anyway? Humming to the beat pounding in her ears, she bent over the trunk and picked up the first object: a Santa Luisa High School class ring. Without the usual blue stone. And . . . her red leather key case! What was that doing here? Beside it lay a paper napkin, pale blue, exactly like the ones Trudy had brought to her birthday party. Her initials swirled across one corner: T.S. The tiniest traces of chocolate cookie crumbs clung to one edge.

A pulse in Tess's throat began to beat double-time, out of synchronization with the drums pounding through her headphones.

Then she saw one more object: a large, fat, purple Magic Marker.

She stood stock-still in the corner of the room, holding the key case in her hands.

After a minute, she remembered that she was wearing the same red top she'd worn to the party. Reaching into one pocket, she pulled out the blue gem she'd found in the sand. She placed it carefully into the hollow of the ring on the trunk.

It fit perfectly. As she had known it would.

What did all this stuff mean? What was it doing lying there so neatly, so well-ordered, like . . . like . . .

"It's like a shrine," she said aloud, lifting the earphones from her head as she picked up the ring to look for initials inside it.

"Well, good for *you*," a voice said from directly behind her. The headphones had prevented her from hearing footsteps on the attic stairs.

"Because that's exactly what it is," the voice, hoarse from stomach-pump tubes, said. "A shrine. To my mother, actually."

Tess whirled to meet the voice.

It belonged to her brother, Guy Joe Landers, Jr.

Chapter 26

A thoroughly bewildered Tess looked up at Guy Joe. "A shrine? To our mother?"

It was amazing then, the way his face changed, twisted into something strange and terrifying, his gray eyes cold with contempt, his upper lip raised in an ugly sneer. "Not *our* mother, stupid! *My* mother!" Then, more calmly, he added, "We didn't have the same one, you know."

"Guy Joe, what are you talking about? Of course we did!"

He shook his head. "That's what *you* think. I know better." He leaned forward, grabbing one of her wrists and clutching it tightly. "They *stole* me," he hissed in her face, "stole me right out of my mother's arms. And now they're paying for it! And you're going to pay, too. Because it was *your* father who kept the truth from me. He was the one who adopted me and never told me."

Tess felt dizzy. What was he *talking* about? Guy Joe was adopted? He wasn't her real brother? That was crazy. She would have known. Wouldn't she?

Wouldn't *he*? People told adopted children the truth now, didn't they?

But there was something in Guy Joe's eyes that told her he believed every word he was telling her. And it was making him crazy.

Her eyes went to the top of the trunk. The ring, the key case, the napkin with brownie crumbs . . . Guy Joe had put them there. Each of them had something to do with one of the accidents. *Which meant . . . which meant . . .*

"Yes, I did it," he said triumphantly, reading her mind. "I did all of it, and it was easy. So easy! This town is full of fools! Greedy fools. They wouldn't close The Boardwalk because they were afraid of losing a few dollars, so they made it easy for me."

"No, Guy Joe," Tess said softly, "you wouldn't . . ."

"Wouldn't what? Wouldn't kill Dade Lewis and send the others to the hospital? Oh, wouldn't I? It was justice, Tess, pure and simple. They had it coming, all of them. They asked for it. They were all in on it. Your father and his friends. They stole me and then they kept that truth from me. All of them."

"I don't understand." She tried to back away from him, really frightened now. Because she believed him. It hadn't been Doss or Trudy, after all. It had been Guy Joe all along. And now, suddenly, it wasn't safe to be around her own brother. Only . . . only he was telling her now that he *wasn't* her brother. How could that be?

"You don't *have* to understand," he sneered. "All

you have to do is come with me. I have plans for you."

She pulled against his grip on her wrist. "Guy Joe, tell me what this is all about. What's going on? I'm your sister. You can tell me. I won't hate you, I promise."

He laughed, a harsh sound that echoed throughout the attic. "*Sister?* Don't you get it? Weren't you listening? You're not my sister. You're not anybody's sister! Because I'm not your brother. I'm not even a Landers. My real parents were named Lila and Tully O'Hare." He paused and took a deep breath. "And that's all I'm telling you. You don't need to know the whole story. All you have to do is come with me."

"No!" she cried, every instinct telling her he meant her real harm. "I'm not going anywhere with you!"

His hand lashed out and slapped her across the face.

"You will do," he said coldly, "exactly what I tell you to do. You've made enough trouble for me already. Fouling things up in the Funhouse that day! You almost ruined everything."

Tess shifted nervously, eyeing the attic stairs. Could she get to them before he could stop her? Probably not. "What are you going to do?" she asked.

"We're going to have some fun," he said with an evil grin. Then he pushed her ahead of him, toward the stairs. "And if you're thinking of screaming, go right ahead. Maria went home, and your father, in case you've forgotten, is at one of his precious board meetings. So yell your lungs out if you want to."

When they reached the top of the narrow attic stairs, he gave her another push, shoving her down the stairs. He retained his tight grip on her wrist and said casually as he hurried her along, "When we've finished having our fun, we're going to meet my real parents. You'll like them, Tess. They'll be mad at you, at first, because of who your father is, but they'll get over it."

Deciding that the best approach might be to humor Guy Joe until she could think of something else, she said innocently, "Where do your real parents live?"

"Live?" At the top of the wide, curving staircase, he stopped and forced her to face him. "They don't *live*, Tess! Your father and his wicked friends drove both of my real parents to suicide! They're dead!"

Then, as she stared at him in stunned dismay, he added emphatically, "And what was good enough for them is good enough for me. And you, too."

He was talking about two people who had committed suicide. Two people who were dead. He was talking about joining those dead people, and taking her with him.

Tess's knees gave and she slumped against Guy Joe.

He yanked her upright. "Cut it out, Tess!" he said sharply. "Come on, now. I don't have all night. Let's get this show on the road."

Numb with shock and fear, Tess let Guy Joe pull her down the stairs. When he yanked open the front door, windblown rain attacked them. "Can't I grab a jacket?" Tess pleaded. "I'll get soaked!" If he'd let go of her wrist for just a second, she could make a run for it. Sam's house wasn't that far away. Sam. How could she ever have suspected Sam?

Guy Joe snickered and pushed her out onto the porch. "You're worried about getting wet? You really are stupid!"

When he'd shoved her inside his car and taken the wheel, he used his electronic control to lock her door. Then he yanked her seat belt across her chest, and snapped it into place. "If you try to unhook it," he warned as he started the car, "I'll break your arm."

She knew he meant it. Just as she knew he'd been telling the truth about being adopted. How had he found out? Why hadn't someone told him a long time ago? Wouldn't that be a horrible thing to learn when you were eighteen years old? Like . . . like your whole life wasn't what you thought it was. It would be a terrible shock, wouldn't it? In Guy Joe's case, it must have been enough of a shock to send him over the edge.

Her mind felt fuzzy, as if it were wrapped in cotton. She *had* to think, but she couldn't.

"You pushed me into Trudy's pool?" she asked, shivering in her seat.

He nodded, peering into the rain-slicked windshield.

"And the brownies, you did that, too? And then ate some, so no one would suspect you, right?"

"Clever, huh?" he said. "Miserable experience,"

he added, shaking his head. "But necessary."

"The saucer. How did you get the saucer up? And what did you do with it after you took it out?"

He laughed, obviously enjoying himself. "Those things wear out so fast they have to be replaced a lot. So they're easy to lift up and out. A baby could do it. The one I took was right there under your feet the whole time. I just slid it onto the one beside it. Afterward I said I was going to call Gina's parents, and on the way I slipped into the Funhouse and replaced the saucer."

Tess remembered the humiliating walk to Mancini's office, and burned with rage. She made one last, desperate attempt to reason with him. "Guy Joe, I don't know how you found out what you think you found out, but you could be wrong. And even if you're right, it doesn't matter to *me* that you're adopted. I mean, I'll always think of you as my —"

Before she could finish he had slammed on the brakes. "It matters to *me!*" he shouted. "You stupid, selfish little witch, it matters to me! If you don't understand anything else before you die, understand that!"

When they arrived at The Boardwalk and he had pulled her out into the parking lot, she felt a sudden surge of hope. She might see someone she knew, someone who could help her.

But the amusement park was deserted. Attendants in the booths and the arcades, passing the boring hours reading or watching tiny portable televisions, never even looked up as Guy Joe dragged her toward the Funhouse. No one paid the slightest attention to them.

Except Doss Beecham, who looked up from the high stool he was sitting on in one of the shooting galleries. But when he saw who was passing by, he barely nodded. She couldn't blame him, after the way she'd treated him. He looked unusually pale after his ordeal of the night before. If only she could signal him that Guy Joe had been behind all of it. But Doss was no longer looking her way.

"Don't you even *look* at him!" Guy Joe ordered under his breath. "He can't help you."

Maybe if she'd been nicer to Doss, he would know her well enough to sense that something was wrong, and come to her rescue.

Too late now.

Too late, too late, too late . . .

The attendant in the ticket booth for the Funhouse never took his eyes off the baseball game on his portable television as Guy Joe quickly paid for two admissions and pushed Tess ahead of him.

"Go ahead and scream," Guy Joe said cheerfully when they were inside the empty Funhouse. "Screaming in here doesn't mean a thing. No one will even notice."

She knew he was right. And now she was alone in this dark and frightening place with someone who had caused the death of one person and had hurt a lot of others. And there was no one to help her.

"Take your shoes off!" he commanded.

"What? Guy Joe, I can't go through the Funhouse in my bare feet. It's hard enough with sneakers on."

He laughed. "You're so stupid. You're worried about your *feet*?"

She waited, knowing instinctively that she wasn't going to like what was coming.

"Tess," he said softly, his cold eyes on hers, "didn't I make myself clear?" He stooped to untie and slip off first one of her sneakers and a sock, then the other, using only one hand. His free hand imprisoned her ankle as he performed his task.

When she was barefoot, he stood up, recapturing her arm. "Little ex-sister," he said in that same soft voice, "this Funhouse is the last place your feet will ever touch."

He smiled down at her. "Because this is where you're going to die."

Chapter 27

As they came out of the dark entryway into the first lighted chamber, Tess fought desperately against Guy Joe's grip, tears of frustration and fear streaking her face. "No!" she screamed as he dragged her into the nylon-padded tunnel with the rolling wooden floor. "No, Guy Joe, *stop!*"

But he ignored her, pushing and pulling at her until her bare feet slid onto the rolling boards.

She tried to plant herself firmly in one spot, but without shoes it was impossible. Clutching at the billowing black nylon fabric that made up the tunnel's sides was equally useless. The loose, black, silky folds waved this way and that, eluding her grasp.

Feeling like a helpless puppet, she continued to struggle. Guy Joe stood on the wooden walkway, watching her, amusement on his face. "I don't know exactly where my father died," he said in a friendly voice, "so I'll just have to pick my own spot. But first," he added with a wicked grin, "we'll have some fun. Isn't that why they call this place the Funhouse?" He chuckled, a sound that sent shivers of fear down Tess's spine.

"Guy Joe, please . . ."

"Guy-Joe-please, Guy-Joe-please," he mimicked cruelly. "Please what?" He stared at her, his upper lip curled in a menacing sneer. "Is there something you *want*, Tess?"

As Tess tried to cross the chamber, she fell twice, landing first on her back, then on her elbows, smacking them sharply against the wood. Guy Joe laughed each time. When she had finally made her way across, she stepped onto the solid wood floor to find Guy Joe waiting for her. He pushed her onward.

The padded rolling tunnel was next. Her bare feet slid on the nylon fabric underneath them. She was tossed to the floor repeatedly as the tunnel bucked from side to side. She felt dizzy, her head was pounding, and her whole body ached from falling down.

"Guy Joe," she gasped as she fell again, "why are you *doing* this? I never knew you were adopted. I would have told you if I'd known. I wasn't keeping anything secret from you."

"I'm doing it because you're *his* child!" he shouted. "His real child! Can't you see that I'm really punishing him, or are you too dense to make the connection?"

"But he's not even *here*," she argued. "He doesn't know anything about this!"

"Ah, but he will." Guy Joe smiled angelically. "It's all in a journal I left behind. Everything that's happened is in there, including our little adventure in here. In graphic detail. He'll know what fun we had before the end."

The end? She didn't want to die.

"Now get up!" he shouted, angry again. "Quit stalling!"

She stayed where she was. Why should she make it easy for him? She stretched out on her stomach, full-length, on the tunnel's padded floor. Let him come and get her. Maybe in a struggle, she could somehow get the upper hand.

"I've decided to hang both of us from those two skeletons in the middle chamber," he said, friendly again, as if they were planning an outing. "Won't that be a hoot for whoever finds us?"

"*Hang* us?"

"Sure. Like father, like son, right? My father did it. Said so in his obituary. I looked it up at the library. Didn't say where, exactly. The writer was too squeamish, I guess. So I get to pick the place. And I choose the skeletons." Taking a penknife from his back pocket, he ripped a long, narrow strip of nylon from the tunnel's side. Then he tore a second strip and stuffed it into the pocket, along with the knife.

Suddenly, without warning, he jumped onto the padding and grabbed Tess, looping the nylon strip around her neck.

"Now get up!" he commanded, tugging on the strip around her neck. "Or I'll finish you off right here!"

They entered the chain-walk tunnel.

"Guy Joe," she croaked, the nylon pulling too

tightly on her throat, "I can't go across those chains in my bare feet. I can't!"

Still holding the nylon strip in one hand, Guy Joe gave her a shove, sending her onto the links. Balancing properly was impossible and she fell again and again into the meshed circle of metal links.

"See," Guy Joe said happily, "what I'm going to do is tie this end of your rope to that hook the skeleton dangles from. You'll be standing on the railing when I do that."

Tess tried desperately to grip the metal with her toes. It was impossible. Down she went again, slicing one of her toes as she fell. She cried out, but Guy Joe ignored her and went on talking.

"Then you'll jump," he went on matter-of-factly. "Bye-bye, Tess, easy as that. Then it'll be my turn. Isn't it nice that there's one skeleton hook for each of us?"

"I won't jump!" Tess cried. "I won't!"

Guy Joe shrugged. "Okay. You don't have to. I'll just push you."

He meant it. She knew that. Whatever Guy Joe had learned about himself, it had stolen the brother she knew and replaced him with this person who had no conscience, no qualms whatsoever about taking her life and his own. She *had* to do something to stop him.

Tess struggled across the remaining chains. When she was on the wooden platform, she said, "I can't walk, Guy Joe. I've cut my foot."

Guy Joe bent to glance down at her foot, giving Tess just enough time to grasp the chain belt at her waist, unsnapping the clasp. In one smooth motion, she yanked the metal belt free from its loops and swung hard, whipping it down across the back of Guy Joe's head.

Stunned, he fell to his knees, releasing his end of the rope.

Tess ran. She raced into the next chamber, where the metal saucers whirled. She knew she had only a second or two. Bending quickly, she reached down with both hands and, stretching her arms across, grabbed at the middle circle and pulled upward. It came up out of the floor easily, just as Guy Joe had said.

She heard footsteps behind her. Lifting the circle, using what little strength she had left, she tossed it into the next passageway. It landed with a sharp clink and then fell silent.

Tess ran across the wooden walkway to the opposite side of the circles. Then, swinging the chain belt with careful aim, she smashed the overhead light in the ceiling, throwing the tunnel into absolute darkness. She crouched there, trembling violently, waiting.

"I'll get you for this, Tess Landers!" Guy Joe's voice, full of rage, cried as he entered the tunnel. "You'll be very—"

He never finished the threat. Consumed with rage and blinded by the sudden, unexpected darkness, his voice became a scream of terror as the hole Tess had created swallowed him up.

Chapter 28

Tess would hear Guy Joe's scream in her sleep for many nights to come.

Crouching in the corner, trembling violently, she covered her face with her hands.

"Tess! Tess, where are you?" Tess heard a voice cry out, frantic with worry. *Sam.*

"Here! I'm here! Be careful — there's a saucer missing!"

In spite of the darkness, Sam made his way across the chamber, and a moment later he was kneeling at her side. "You okay?" Lifting her gently, he put his arms around her.

"How did you know I was here?"

"Gina. She called me. She got this weird package at the hospital today. From Guy Joe. A couple of journals. One was his and the other one was an old one, written by some woman." Sam began leading Tess out of the Funhouse, using one of the wooden walkways. The rain had stopped, and the half moon cast a faint glow over the beach. "I didn't have any idea what she was talking about, but she was scared. For you. She told me to find you, right away. I'd just hung up when Doss called me and said you and Guy Joe were here and that Guy Joe looked funny, sort of freaked out. So here I am."

So Doss *had* noticed something strange, after all. And hadn't ignored it. She would have to remember to thank him.

"Where's Guy Joe?" Sam asked.

"Down there." Tess pointed to a spot on the beach. Guy Joe was unconscious. He looked so helpless, so innocent, lying there on the sand, that Tess found it hard to believe that tonight's horror had actually happened. "We'd better call another ambulance. But," Tess added softly, "this will be the last one."

Epilogue

They think I'm unconscious. But I heard every word they said. Dr. Oliver said to that man who's *supposed* to be my father, "We've had our hands full lately with these kids, haven't we? Buddy Slaughter tells me Trudy is just about hysterical after what happened at her birthday party."

I had finally found out what I'd been afraid I'd never know. Trudy's father was the "Buddy" Lila had written about. The only one who hadn't suffered at my hands.

Okay. No sweat. I'd go wherever they sent me. I'd weave little baskets and play Ping-Pong with the other loonies and I'd talk to the shrinks.

But I'd get out some day. And when I did, the eighth man on the board would be waiting. Buddy Slaughter, the man who had stolen everything from me, would be waiting.

So I could wait, too. . . .

About the Author

DIANE HOH grew up in Warren, Pennsylvania, "a lovely small town on the Allegheny River." Since then, she has lived in New York State, Colorado, and North Carolina. Ten years ago, she and her family settled in Austin, Texas, where they plan to stay. "Reading and writing take up most of my life," says Ms. Hoh, "along with family, music, and gardening."

point® **THRILLERS**

R.L. Stine

- ☐ MC44236-8 The Baby-sitter — $3.50
- ☐ MC44332-1 The Baby-sitter II — $3.50
- ☐ MC45386-6 Beach House — $3.25
- ☐ MC43278-8 Beach Party — $3.50
- ☐ MC43125-0 Blind Date — $3.50
- ☐ MC43279-6 The Boyfriend — $3.50
- ☐ MC44333-X The Girlfriend — $3.50
- ☐ MC45385-8 Hit and Run — $3.25
- ☐ MC46100-1 The Hitchhiker — $3.50
- ☐ MC43280-X The Snowman — $3.50
- ☐ MC43139-0 Twisted — $3.50

Caroline B. Cooney

- ☐ MC44316-X The Cheerleader — $3.25
- ☐ MC41641-3 The Fire — $3.25
- ☐ MC43806-9 The Fog — $3.25
- ☐ MC45681-4 Freeze Tag — $3.25
- ☐ MC45402-1 The Perfume — $3.25
- ☐ MC44884-6 The Return of the Vampire — $2.95
- ☐ MC41640-5 The Snow — $3.25
- ☐ MC45682-2 The Vampire's Promise — $3.50

Diane Hoh

- ☐ MC44330-5 The Accident — $3.25
- ☐ MC45401-3 The Fever — $3.25
- ☐ MC43050-5 Funhouse — $3.25
- ☐ MC44904-4 The Invitation — $3.50
- ☐ MC45640-7 The Train (9/92) — $3.25

Sinclair Smith

- ☐ MC45063-8 The Waitress — $2.95

Christopher Pike

- ☐ MC43014-9 Slumber Party — $3.50
- ☐ MC44256-2 Weekend — $3.50

A. Bates

- ☐ MC45829-9 The Dead Game — $3.25
- ☐ MC43291-5 Final Exam — $3.25
- ☐ MC44582-0 Mother's Helper — $3.50
- ☐ MC44238-4 Party Line — $3.25

D.E. Athkins

- ☐ MC45246-0 Mirror, Mirror — $3.25
- ☐ MC45349-1 The Ripper — $3.25
- ☐ MC44941-9 Sister Dearest — $2.95

Carol Ellis

- ☐ MC44768-8 My Secret Admirer — $3.25
- ☐ MC46044-7 The Stepdaughter — $3.25
- ☐ MC44916-8 The Window — $2.95

Richie Tankersley Cusick

- ☐ MC43115-3 April Fools — $3.25
- ☐ MC43203-6 The Lifeguard — $3.25
- ☐ MC43114-5 Teacher's Pet — $3.25
- ☐ MC44235-X Trick or Treat — $3.25

Lael Littke

- ☐ MC44237-6 Prom Dress — $3.25

Edited by T. Pines

- ☐ MC45256-8 Thirteen — $3.50

Available wherever you buy books, or use this order form.

Scholastic Inc., P.O. Box 7502, 2931 East McCarty Street, Jefferson City, MO 65102

Please send me the books I have checked above. I am enclosing $_____ (please add $2.00 to cover shipping and handling). Send check or money order — no cash or C.O.D.s please.

Name _____

Address_____

City_____ State/Zip_____

Please allow four to six weeks for delivery. Offer good in the U.S. only. Sorry, mail orders are not available to residents of Canada. Prices subject to change.   PT1092

THRILLERS